Praise for *Acts of Service*

"This one had me hooked from the first sentence. . . . Lillian Fishman has written one of the most entertaining books about sex I've ever read. Like any good dating experience, it's heady, exhilarating, and will change the way you look at the world. The perfect read for fans of Raven Leilani and Ottessa Moshfegh, this is a book that will have people talking."

—*BuzzFeed*

"A fun debut novel that feels like the life story of half of Brooklyn." —*Nylon*

"Smart in its triangulations and tensions, and on the question of how a certain set of politically minded young people are supposed to live now."

—*The New York Times Book Review*

"A young woman follows her exhibitionist streak to uncharted new territory in this bold and unflinchingly sexy novel, engaging in a three-way sexual relationship that teaches her more than she could have imagined about her own desire."

—*Vogue*

"A radical understanding of the multi-hyphenate definitions of sexual orientation . . . Using sex as a road map, Eve is searching to understand her own inner workings as a young woman. We tend to love what disturbs us, if we are willing to follow our desires and take the risk." —*Interview*

"Conversational, frank, and canny." —*Glamour*

"Ottessa Moshfegh's urban malaise meets Raven Leilani's loquacious eroticism in this provocative novel."
—*Electric Literature*

"[Eve's] adventure, she realizes, presents all the issues that preoccupy her—"desire, sex, gender, attention, intimacy, vanity, and power"—in such a way that she can "study them like fruit in a bowl." —*The New Yorker*

"Searching and enthralling . . . Part erotic *Bildungsroman,* part melancholy comedy of manners, it arrives with quiet confidence and a fully formed bank of ideas about intimacy, sexual ethics and contemporary mores that Fishman could go on exploring for years to come." —*The New Statesman*

"A new kind of queer novel . . . razor-sharp hedonism, and Fishman's characters lean into the granular pleasures of sex at the expense of a moral compass." —*The Cut*

"This one might be my top pick for Hot Girl Book of the year. . . . a messy, whirlwind relationship that tests all the boundaries of coercion and consent. It's in these murky grey areas that Lillian Fishman's writing thrives, asking readers: How much of sex is said out loud, and what does it mean when it's not?" —*BookPeople* blog

"A modern-day exploration of sexuality, ethics, and consent." —*Bustle*

"A smart, sexy novel, *Acts of Service* tackles modern sexual dynamics with a refreshing frankness. As Olivia is increasingly sexually liberated, she begins to wrestle with ideas of what society tells her she should want versus what she actually wants." —*Nonchalant*

"Themes of sexuality, queerness, desire, consent, gender, and narcissism saturate this sexy novel that's as ponderous as it is erotic, titillating, and dangerous . . . a standout." —*Bay Area Reporter*

"A smart and extremely current interrogation of queerness and modern sexual ethics, populated with intriguingly complex characters, all told in an enthralling voice." —*Powells Books* blog

"A perfectly messy inquiry into the nature of power and desire." —*Chicago Review of Books*

"[A] provocative, daring read." —*Electric Lit*

"Thrilling." —*The Millions*

"I was completely absorbed by this radical, daring and bracing novel about a so-cold and yet so-intimate world where safety and pleasure can only be found in the most unlikely and unpredictable of places. It is a book of exciting, provocative complexity, and, for me, it made the human creature feel like something new." —Sheila Heti, author of *Pure Color*

"*Acts of Service* doesn't kiss you first, it gets right to it—depicting the liquid frequencies of need and power with a thoughtful, savage eye." —Raven Leilani, author of *Luster*

"Fascinating . . . a book of exquisite moral refinement and almost intimidating elegance." —Edmund White, author of *A Boy's Own Story* and *States of Desire*

"*Acts of Service* doesn't shy away from asking big questions about the nature of attraction. All this, but with a great deal of page-turning pleasure." —Gary Shteyngart, author of *Our Country Friends* and *Super Sad Love Love Story*

"A kind of supercharged combo of Sally Rooney and Ottessa Moshfegh, and as smart as Joan Didion, Fishman isn't just a brilliant writer—she's a brilliant feeler, a great thinker. She has the gift we open books for." —David Lipsky, author of *The Art Fair*

"Months after turning the final page, I'm still thinking about this fiercely wily novel." —Heidi Julavits, author of *The Folded Clock*

ABOUT THE TYPE

This book was set in Minion, a 1990 Adobe Originals typeface by Robert Slimbach (b. 1956). Minion is inspired by classical, old-style typefaces of the late Renaissance, a period of elegant, beautiful, and highly readable type designs. Created primarily for text setting, Minion combines the aesthetic and functional qualities that make text type highly readable with the versatility of digital technology.

ACTS of SERVICE

ACTS
OF
SERVICE

A Novel

LILLIAN FISHMAN

HOGARTH
London • New York

Published in the United States by Hogarth, an imprint of Random House, a division of Penguin Random House LLC, New York.

HOGARTH is a trademark of the Random House Group Limited, and the H colophon is a trademark of Penguin Random House LLC.

Originally published in hardcover in the United States by Hogarth, an imprint of Random House, a division of Penguin Random House LLC, in 2022.

Library of Congress Cataloging-in-Publication Data
Names: Fishman, Lillian, author.
Title: Acts of service: a novel / Lillian Fishman.
Description: New York: Hogarth, 2022.
Identifiers: LCCN 2021023253 (print) | LCCN 2021023254 (ebook) |
ISBN 9780593243787 (paperback) | ISBN 9780593243770 (ebook)
Subjects: LCSH: Lesbians—Fiction. | Triangles (Interpersonal relations)—Fiction. |
LCGFT: Erotic fiction. | Novels.
Classification: LCC PS3606.I843 A65 2022 (print) | LCC PS3606.I843 (ebook) |
DDC 813/.6——dc23
LC record available at https://lccn.loc.gov/2021023253
LC ebook record available at https://lccn.loc.gov/2021023254

Export ISBN 978-0-593-44621-8

Printed in the United States of America on acid-free paper

randomhousebooks.com

1st Printing

He had said, "You won't write a book about me." But I haven't written a book about him, neither have I written a book about myself. All I have done is translate into words—words he will probably never read; they are not intended for him—the way in which his existence has affected my life. An offering of a sort, bequeathed to others.

ANNIE ERNAUX, *SIMPLE PASSION*

ACTS OF SERVICE

PART I

Attention

1

I had hundreds of nudes stored in my phone, but I'd never sent them to anyone. The shots themselves were fairly standard: my faceless body floating in bedrooms and bathrooms, in mirrors. Whenever I took one I fell in love with it for a moment. Standing there, naked and hunched over my little screen, I felt overwhelmed with the urge to show someone this new iteration of my body. But each photo seemed more private and impossible than the last.

You could see in them something beyond desire, harder and more humiliating. While I was brushing my teeth or stepping out of the shower I would see my own body and find myself overwhelmed with a sense of urgency and disuse. My body was crying out that I was not fulfilling my purpose. I was meant to have sex—probably with some wild number of people. Maybe it was more savage than that, that I was meant not to fuck but to get fucked. The purpose of my life at large remained mysterious, but I had come around to the idea that my purpose as a body was simple.

I was too fearful of the world to go out and get fucked, too plagued by hang-ups, memories of shitty girlfriends, fears of violence. Instead I took photos. In the photos my body looked stunning, unblemished, often arched as though trying to escape the top of the frame. I was like a spinster full of anxieties and repressions, charged with chaperoning a young girl who could not fathom the injustice of the arrangement.

One night when I was feeling exceptionally beautiful and isolated I decided to start sharing the nudes online. I used a website that anonymized usernames and disguised IP addresses, and I put up three photos with no accompanying text.

———

I was on my girlfriend's toilet, the next morning, when Olivia messaged me. My post had accumulated more responses than I could possibly read. Perhaps it shouldn't have come as a surprise that none of the lewdness, the appreciation, not even the occasional brutality of these comments satisfied me. The anonymity of the photos felt cowardly, the distance of the viewers so great as to make their sentiments meaningless. The only part that thrilled me was repeatedly refreshing the page to see the photos reconstitute themselves again and again, not in a private folder on my phone but in a shared white room accessible from all corners of the world.

I was guilty of some trespass against my girlfriend, Romi—that was clear from the fact that I was refreshing the page while hiding in her bathroom. Romi's drugstore-brand cleanser was perched on the sink. Her clean hospital scrubs hung on the back of the door like a poor drawing of a person. But, I reasoned, looking down at my phone, the photos had nothing to do with her. It was only my body that appeared in them, and my body didn't belong to her.

What would Romi do if I showed her the photos? She'd be a little sad, a little confused. *What can I do?* she would say, convinced that only some inadequacy of hers could leave me wanting the affirmation of strangers.

I assumed the vast majority of the responses were from men. Their comments were full of typos and references to their erections. I smiled, scrolled. When I refreshed again the message at the top was from a user called *paintergirl1992*. I read the words in the preview—*Excuse me*—and stifled a laugh.

Excuse me, the message read, *I'm sorry to intrude! Your photos are very beautiful. Thank you for sharing. I would love to buy you a drink—are you in NY? Sorry to be so forward. I hope you have a lovely day—Olivia*

olivia, I replied, *where do you live in ny?*

Baby? Romi said loudly from the hall. Are you okay in there?

I'm fine, I said.

Olivia was replying in real time.

Clinton Hill, Olivia wrote. *BK! Are you in NY too?*

ya

Would you like to meet?

who are you

Olivia sent a link to a social-media profile.

Do you want some coffee? Romi called through the door.

I opened Olivia's profile. I didn't know what to think. I put down my phone and yelled, Yes, over the flush of the toilet.

—

You can see why I didn't trust myself. There was no reason, in the first place, that I should feel so beautiful and isolated. I had a lovely girlfriend—selfless, adoring, great in bed, with the strong arms and shoulders produced by years of rugby. Yet for reasons that were still unclear to me I had uploaded the photos the previous evening while sitting only two feet away from her, after dinner, while she answered some emails.

The only thing I was clear on was why I had never shown Romi the photos. Romi was the noblest person I had ever met. I liked extreme people, people who seemed to embody an unambiguous idea about life. What would it feel like to be unwaveringly good? The poles of Romi's nobility were her self-sacrificing nature and her absolute insusceptibility to the superficial. From a young age, she had prized a sense of competence and the belief that she was capable of making a significant social contribution. After toying with the possibility of a political career, she had decided to pursue pediatrics. In her off-hours she volunteered as an EMT.

She was so preoccupied with her vocation that she was immune to beauty. The concept hadn't occurred to her outside an introductory art-history course. Her choices were made on the basis of function. The building she lived in was expensive and tasteless, full of beige amenities. Aside from the special uniforms required for exercise or job interviews, every piece of clothing she owned had been picked up for free at some athletic tournament or at the annual reunion for which her fit, cheerful family ordered matching polos. She ate sandwiches and salads and she ate them exclusively at chain restaurants.

Her consistency was perfect. She'd decided she was attracted to me even before she had any idea what I looked like—when all she knew about me, as I liked to joke later on, was that I was a woman with an excellent memory for the names of novelists whose work I'd never read. We had met two years earlier on a crossword app that matched users of comparable ability. Romi was much better than I was at the crossword, but she was hampered by little free time and an aversion to competitive spite. As we chatted over a few months I found I liked the generosity of Romi's messages—even when I failed spectacularly, she never teased me—and she endeared herself to me with the general bent of her knowledge, which was always embarrassing in areas of art or pop culture but acute with regard to politics, history, and the crucial art of synonyms. It felt lucky that she was a young gay woman, only five years older than I was and separated from me by only about a mile.

She didn't love me for my body, though once we were intimate she claimed to recognize a special beauty in it. I didn't believe her. She wasn't discerning. The rapport we'd created online was the clear basis of Romi's affection. Because I was decidedly superficial, and always had been—nothing interested me more than the prettiness of a girl on the street—a small but relentless part of my life entailed predicting the many ways I could fuck up our love. If I was going to deserve her I would have to remain as attentive as she was, as sexually generous, as loyal. Needless to say, I would have to avoid posting my nudes online.

But beyond Romi my desire was thirsty and fickle. I was neither loyal nor anarchic but, unable to decide between the two, guilty and scheming. The primary fantasy that followed me everywhere was a vision in which I was naked, lined up in a row of twenty girls, a hundred girls, as many naked girls as would fit inside the room I was in—the café, the lobby of Romi's building, the subway car. Opposite the line of girls was a man who scrutinized us. I can't tell you what this man looked like. He was nondescript, symbolic. I would never actually fuck him. After about thirty seconds he pointed, without equivocating, at me.

———

It was Sunday. My shift at the café started at seven-thirty. Despite the hour, Romi always made the fifteen-minute walk with me on the weekends. She rinsed our coffee mugs, tucked an apple and a chocolate bar into my bag, retrieved two umbrellas from the floor by the door. There were no hooks or pieces of furniture on which to hang coats or deposit umbrellas; after two years in this apartment, Romi had acquired little beyond standing lamps and a few implements for cooking. In the living room there was a lone coffee table and a small pile of political biographies stacked below the window.

Want your own umbrella? she asked. Or would you like to share?

She walked next to me in the early half-light, holding the single large umbrella over the two of us. A mild snowfall had begun in the night. Around Romi I had this feeling, when she walked me to work or cooked for me or carried my bag—the certainty that my life would be witnessed, safe, warm. I would not suffer small frustrations; I would be protected from the blights of life by love, as a child is protected by love. Like the best heroes and most honorable lovers, Romi would perform not just these small acts but any extravagant, necessary sacrifice on my behalf. As for me—what would I sacrifice? While my arm swung beside Romi's I felt my deception physically, like a mark, and wondered at the fact that Romi couldn't see it.

We were talking, as we sometimes did, about what our lives had been like ten or twelve years earlier, long before we met. We shared a special feeling that queer people imagine belongs to them, the sense that our first experiences with other girls had led us to each other—that as young women we had stumbled through a trapdoor into a small, bright place and found each other among the few other souls who had also managed to discover it.

It was always fraught back then, Romi said. Difficult. My girlfriend didn't want us to have sex, so we never intended to, we would just be hanging out and we'd be kissing and then—you know, something would happen. I never planned it. I didn't even think about it when we weren't together—it wasn't like that. It would just be so intense to be around her, I'd end up touching her, asking her if it was okay. Absolutely yes, she'd say, yes, great, okay.

And then she'd be upset afterward?

No, Romi said, laughing. Afterward she'd say, Well, that isn't sex. So every time we'd get further and further, doing something she had said before we couldn't do. And afterward she'd say it didn't matter, it wasn't sex, anyway. And of course, by the end, we were obviously having sex. I mean, I was really fucking her! Fucking her with my hand, going down on her. Half the time I thought I was just humoring her, going along with this idea that there was some other frontier. And then half the time I was thinking—what was I missing? That we weren't doing? Because I thought it was pretty great.

Romi took my bag and slung it over her shoulder. A lone man in a parka passed us, trailed by two dogs turned spiky and luminescent in the snow. I marveled at Romi in her running shoes and down shell. No gloves, no scarf. She didn't have any interest in accommodating the weather, or perhaps she had complete faith in her own impervious stamina.

The thing I worried about, I suppose, Romi said slowly, was that there was something wrong about the way I looked at her.

Not with the sex itself but—I don't know—the fact that I wanted it, that I thought about it sometimes when I looked at her a certain way. It didn't really bother me that I was gay as much as that I might be creepy, you know, the way a man is creepy.

But you aren't that way at all. Not even when it's called for, I said, teasing.

Romi smiled. The girlfriend she was talking about had been her first, a relationship of eight years. This ex was the only girl Romi had ever been with aside from me; in this way there was something innocent and small-town about her. The only real experience she'd had of her sexuality, of any relationship, was that terrifying first, in which every desire and act seems to determine who you'll be for the rest of your life. But this very innocence drew me to her, even now, as she spoke. I could feel the gravity of that period in her memory.

For me, I said, it was sort of the opposite. As soon as we had sex—the girl I was with in high school—we didn't even really have sex, you know, we were just fooling around. But she came, and she hadn't realized she was going to, since we were still in our clothes. Maybe she had never even come before. As soon as it happened, it was like she saw something she hadn't been willing to see. She couldn't look away from it. We both knew what it was, and we hadn't known it was going to be like that. That moment shocked us both. And that was the end of it.

Back then, I remembered, watching our boots in the slush, I had felt as though sex were an oracle. A truth-teller just waiting to find me out.

——

At work I checked my phone every hour in the bathroom. I scrolled down, past the new comments and message requests, to

Olivia's. The profile she had sent looked real. Certainly the fact that the page dated back five years suggested that it wasn't the work of someone who periodically created and deleted suspect profiles. But there was also something unselfconscious about it, a lack of vanity, even a kind of visible shyness. Olivia was short and narrow, with a massive cloud of curly hair that made her bookish face look delicate. She wore black and navy—modest high-necked dresses and expensive triple-ply sweaters. She was an enthusiastic documenter of animals, home-baking projects, and the concerts of bedroom-pop singers, some of whom I liked but would have shied from ever mentioning online. It was hard for me to imagine someone creating a fake profile with pictures of such a desexualized, earnest person, and yet it was just as hard to imagine this girl, in real life, not only looking at the anonymous nudes board but mustering the boldness to send me a message. Then again—wasn't it the apologetic formality of her note that had piqued my interest?

By two P.M. she had agreed to meet me for a drink the following night in Bed-Stuy.

———

That evening I moved stiffly through the familiar spaces of my life, like an unwitting participant of a game show who has only just realized she is on camera. When I got off work Romi arrived with her large umbrella and a cookie. Though it was still afternoon the air was deepening. As we walked to her place I was quiet, a hollow feeling in my stomach. We rode the elevator up in silence. The chime startled me when we reached the twelfth floor. I looked at my phone, but it was blank.

Let's fool around, I said when Romi opened the door to her apartment. I started to remove my boots and clothes and pile them on the floor. I was hiding in a costume and I felt a hot need to shed it. Romi smiled and disappeared into the bathroom to arrange the strap-on. She always liked to change in private; there was a quietude in our relationship, the sense that talk of sex might pollute its purity.

In Romi's bedroom the mattress rested directly on the carpet, its only companion a large stainless-steel water bottle. I lay down, looking at my body. I had tried to picture Olivia's body under those high-necked sweaters. Boyish, childish even. I wondered if Olivia would find my body perfect. Hadn't she already? But would she like its shape in person, its size and weight, its responses? Why did I even want to meet her? I couldn't believe that she would be aggressive or demanding, the way I envisioned the man who presided over the lineup in my fantasy. It was her polite mildness that had allowed me to shrug off my fear and make a date with her in the first place. What, then? Was it simply that she was someone who had chosen me for my beauty, for no reason but my beauty, as though that was enough?

Romi came into the room in a white T-shirt. The dildo hung at her hip like an arm. She dimmed the light, moving with hesitant purpose, as though she was preparing to do something about which she felt determined but that was not natural to her. Her body was solid and so fully her own that it didn't need to be invented by sex. As she knelt on the mattress I turned toward her and opened every muscle I had.

She fucked me the way she liked to: as though we'd been apart. She teased the moment of entrance as long as she could. Softly I started to talk, to persuade her to talk to me. I wanted to expand the realm of things made pure by her. Tell me what's happening right now, I said into her ear. Tell me how your cock feels. Tell me what I look like. She said *baby*, just *baby*. The room grew dark and blue, the air humid, as though we had breathed a new season of our own into being. I felt myself near tears. I was so engulfed that I couldn't distinguish whether it was the swell of pleasure or heartbreak. I held Romi against me tightly. Her breasts were large on her athlete's frame, usually hidden behind sports bras or binders. On her back, under her shirt, sweat had begun to rise beneath my hands. The revelation of her body, stripped of its pretenses, was no longer a revelation but a reminder of a choice I made again and again, of a safety represented by Romi's arms.

When I came it felt like a tremendous cough, as though my body were failing to expel a stone lodged inside it.

—

The apartment I shared with my friend Fatima was a fifteen-minute walk from Romi's. In the years Fatima and I had lived in our little two-bedroom we had accumulated too many pieces of mismatched furniture, some with skirts and variously patterned pillows, and a vast collection of plants that Fatima kept alive. The apartment had a sort of musty sweetness to it, a smell of cocoa and linen. We kept the kitchen clear except for an electric kettle on the counter. For years we'd had a little ritual—tea on the couch when we found ourselves at home together.

Fatima was surprised to see me so late. I often stayed at Romi's, where we had the space to ourselves.

How was work? she asked.

Sheepishly, I showed her Olivia's profile.

She's a regular at the café, I lied. She gave me her number today when I rang her up.

But why? Fatima said. I mean, what about Romi?

I can't take a girl's number?

Seems a bit dishonest. Then again—Fatima raised her eyebrows—I know how you like to meet people.

Fatima settled tea bags into two mugs as she spoke. She was a pretty, practical girl who attracted loyal boyfriends. I was both envious of and baffled by her apparently effortless stability. She so often wanted exactly what it seemed she was supposed to want and then enjoyed it once she got it. For example: boyfriends who adored her. At the time she was in love with a programmer named Jeremy.

Well—what do you think of her? I said. Olivia. The girl.

Not your usual type.

Looks straight, you mean?

Yes, Fatima said, laughing as she poured from the kettle. I guess that's what I mean.

I'm in some kind of mood, I said. I don't know.

What do you mean? Is something wrong with you and Romi?

I took the mugs from Fatima and brought them into the living room. I had wanted to talk to someone about Olivia, but now I wished I hadn't brought her up. I didn't like that I had lied to Fatima and omitted the part about the photos, and I liked it even less that she could tell that I was planning something. Worst was that she wasn't surprised.

How do you know, I said to her instead, when you want to sleep with someone?

You know as well as I do.

No, really. Is there something specific? A specific way you know? Or do you not know till they initiate, or till it's happening?

Eve, that's like asking how you knew you were gay.

I laughed. But how *had* I known I was gay? Was I? When I was fifteen I fell in love with a girl I'd grown up with in a tedious town in Massachusetts. Her mother owned a sprawling farm on the north side. We used to spend afternoons in the barn, kissing and tugging at each other's shirts. She was very beautiful, and I knew her better than anyone else. Around her I felt a purpose that I had previously associated with running a distance, knowing I would finish, pulling myself toward a clean triumph, and I understood suddenly the use for which my body had been made. On the evening I described to Romi on our morning walk I had encountered that use and fulfilled it. In the decade since, I had been searching for the return of that exquisite certainty in the rooms and bodies of every girl I knew.

It was beyond me to reconcile what I had felt with its result—that in the wake of her orgasm this girl had given up her friendship with me, all the years we had spent together, the hours spent sputtering in the lake, nights when our flashlights tickled each other's chins, the same hours spent in the same soccer fields, shorts and swimsuits hung in the same bathroom, the same shoes running through the woods on the same path. Maybe it was the case that Olivia looked a little like her.

You know, I said to Fatima, I don't have any idea. I think that first I have to get the thing I want, and maybe then I can figure out why I wanted it, or whether it's good.

2

In college I had discovered a trick to enjoy parties: I would talk to couples, or to pairs who were sleeping together, about the moment in which one of them had seduced the other. *How did you know?* I would ask. I loved watching two people start to laugh over the presumptions they had made, the supreme moment when they realized their feeling was returned. A special look of conspiracy passed between them as they remembered that window of time before sex opened up, the unfolding of the harbored lusts and hopes—the clues, the mechanisms through which they had been discarded and then retrieved. Some people had long, dramatic stories that were designed, in their telling, either to disguise a moral failing or to test the morality of the listener. Other couples revealed that they had slept together within two hours of meeting. Partway through the conversation that look of conspiracy that had moved between them would fall back into each separate face as they remembered the isolation they had felt while they still lived in doubt. There was a portion of all this sweetness that was private, a consolation of a former alienated self.

I was thinking of this when I walked through Bed-Stuy to meet Olivia for the first time—the question of how I would know. Was it simply irrelevant, since we had expressed blunt interest in each other online? There had to be a physical exchange, a look of some kind to reassure us both that our tentative interest remained intact. It had been a couple of years since I had entertained a new flirtation.

When I arrived she was already at the bar, tucked into a corner table and apparently absorbed in a paperback, wearing a long skirt that tickled the floor. Her hair was a thick shroud. She ignored a glass of water.

I touched her shoulder before I sat down, and she started. She had beautiful skin brightened by mild freckles. Her nose was just slightly too wide, and it seemed to make the clouds of her hair appear uncontrolled rather than voluptuous. When she smiled I thought, with shame, of how my own nose threatened to spoil my looks. I was reasonably attractive, but—at least in clothes that hid my body—not strikingly so.

I searched for any sign of disappointment in her expression, but there was only an obliging look, as though she was sorry that she hadn't seen me sooner.

Do you want anything? she said when I had seated myself across from her. A beer or something?

Not yet.

I'm sorry, Olivia said, I don't even know your name. What's your name?

Eve.

She blushed violently, like a middle-school girl. This was not what I had expected from the person who responded to my pictures, and yet it filled me with a warm confidence—the anticipation that I might settle and subdue her, and that she would look up at me with gratitude.

Olivia, I said, I'm glad you messaged me. It was a surprise. But it's nice to meet you.

Why did you pick my message? Olivia said. Or—I suppose you could have responded to plenty of the messages, excuse me.

Are you fishing for a compliment?

No, no, Olivia said, and she pulled the book halfway up toward her chest before catching herself and laying it back face-down on the table.

Well, you can have one, I said. Your hair—it's stunning. I noticed that right away on your profile.

All right, stop, please.

I liked your message too. So polite.

Oh, Olivia said. This time I did see disappointment cross her face—she was ashamed of being liked for her politeness.

What? You know it was polite. I liked that.

Good, she said, without conviction.

And I probably picked it because you're a woman.

Her eyes swung toward the door. I wondered whether it hadn't been a mistake to meet her—whether she was dangerous to me somehow, or even just a girl with little will of her own who had surprised herself by ending up here. I wasn't interested in pure timidity. I had assumed from her message that she was concealing a little wildness.

Does that . . . bother you? I said.

That you preferred a woman's message? Of course not.

What kind of women do you like? I said. You *are* interested in women, right?

Yes, she said.

Are you interested in *me*?

Olivia looked at her lap again. Yes, she said, with the affect of a girl admitting to a petty crime—depositing gum beneath a desk.

Are you? I said.

I didn't mean to insult you, not at all, Olivia said. You're very beautiful. All I mean is that I don't know what I'm interested in—it's all changed—I'm in a strange period of my life, she said suddenly, earnestly.

Okay, I said. What kind of strange period?

It's hard to explain. I don't really talk about it.

What were you interested in before?

I don't know. Art, mostly.

But you're not anymore?

Well, I'm a painter, Olivia said, with an embarrassed tilt of her head, as though she were shrugging off a petting hand. I felt oddly attracted to her tics—the way she disappeared herself beneath her hair, the small frenetic motions she made with her fingers against the spine of the book. Perhaps it was her anxiety I was attracted to—the way it forced me, by contrast, into an unusual ease and confidence.

So you were interested in painting before, I said, and now you're interested in something else. Something sexual, I assume? Since you responded to my photos?

Olivia continued to toy with the book on the table. She shrugged.

What's so strange about your life now?

After a long pause Olivia looked up at me with determined, steadied lips.

There's a man that I'm sleeping with, she said. We liked your pictures, and we thought you might like to meet us. Together.

I was plunged back into that feeling I'd had when I walked

out of the café the day before—the new sense of my life as a spectacle for some lukewarm viewer. There was nothing particularly shocking about Olivia's suggestion. Women who dated other women were familiar with it, even tired of it. But, perhaps out of a desire for intrigue, I felt it as an exciting complication, a new thread to unwind. At the very least it was a confirmation that there was something going on beneath Olivia's shy game. Something preexisting and potentially juicy, subject to its own rules.

Okay, I said. And what makes it strange?

I can't explain. You have to meet him.

Why should I trust you? I mean, who is he?

You'll have to meet him, Olivia said. You'll like him.

Olivia, I said, if that's your name, you sound like you're recruiting me to some kind of cult, do you know that? Whereas I thought I was just on a date with a girl.

Olivia blushed again. There's no cult, she said.

So why didn't you message me together?

We did.

Ah. But you didn't tell me that.

You said just now you preferred messages from women.

Well, why isn't he here?

Our relationship is a bit complicated, Olivia said. We don't go out together very much.

Why not?

I can't explain it all to you myself, Olivia said. But will you meet us? We'd both like to see you. This weekend.

Do you do this often?

Of course not. I've never done it before.

Never asked a woman to meet the two of you? Or never slept with a woman?

No, she said, avoiding my eyes still. No, I've been with a woman before. With women, I mean.

This guy could be anyone.

I know, Olivia said. She smiled finally. I'm not very good at pitching it, am I? Nathan is much better at it than I am. He would convince you in a minute.

How did he convince you?

Oh, no, he didn't convince me, Olivia said. That's a long story.

Well, are you doing anything tonight? Why don't we order some drinks and you tell me the story?

No, I'm sorry. I should go soon. But you should come and meet him this weekend.

It's you I wanted to meet. Besides, I don't trust him.

You don't have any reason to trust me either.

It's true, I said. But I like the way you look. That has to be enough for the moment.

Don't you have any curiosity?

Don't you know men are dangerous?

Be serious, Olivia said gently. Don't you like men, even a little?

You don't have any intuition about men, do you, Fatima had said on one occasion when I went out with her to a straight bar and allowed men to buy me drinks. As though I were an exchange student on her home turf. Yes—the dynamics between men and women were strange. I felt myself trying them on, aware of all the places in which they were not made for me. I could see an inkling of fear in Fatima when I admitted this. I couldn't call what I felt about men *intuition*. Most men seemed hardly to exist for me, except nebulously, as acquaintances or obstacles. And then, occasionally, in the presence of a man who exuded power, I would feel a kind of weightlessness; I could feel myself growing soft and dimpling amiably under even a light touch of his attention. This was a truth so inadmissible in my life that I insisted even to myself that it was not the case.

I don't know, I said to Olivia. I've liked them a few times. But I'd rather not like them any more than I do. I'm not really looking to like them.

Why did you put your pictures up, if you didn't want men to look at them?

I laughed to hide the pain of this observation.

It wasn't a man I agreed to meet, I said again.

No, Olivia said, but I don't think you would mind. I actually think you'll enjoy meeting him a lot.

I liked this too—Olivia's conviction. For the first time she looked certain, or if not certain then at least superior. I was nearing the end of her interest. She was doing this as a favor to the man she mentioned more than out of any desire for me. If I refused her, she would leave only mildly disappointed, with the certainty that it was my loss rather than hers. She and I were in more of an argument than a flirtation, and there had not yet been a moment when I knew for sure that we would, at some point, fall into each other's arms. But right then, glimpsing my own superfluousness, I knew I would try to seduce her.

So I won't get to see you alone? I said. Not at all?

If you'd like to take us up on it, Olivia said, we're free Saturday night. Uptown. I'll text you.

She slipped her coat off the chair and began to gather her things. When she picked up the book I saw it was a fraying copy of *Mansfield Park*.

You're leaving already? I said. That's it?

She looked so ashamed that I immediately regretted having spoken. I was unused to being as delicate as she clearly needed me to be. I still felt affronted by the way the conversation had unfolded.

I'm sorry, she said again. I hope I see you this weekend?

She walked out with her head bowed, skirt drifting behind her.

—

Now that I had come to the edge I wasn't so sure I was ready for it—whatever it was I had found. Up until this point I had spent a lot of time talking myself out of the things I liked so that I could be a different, better kind of person. Over the previous decade I had talked myself all the way from an attraction to women into a political commitment to lesbianism, and all the way from a general pleasure in the indulgences of life into a bitter shame toward all the trifling things I used to enjoy—charm and harmless deceits, intrigues, vanity, pretty women, good dancers, cab rides and coffees out, men who whistled when I passed, remarks that made me blush. Also people who managed to "get away with things," even people who liked to believe they were getting away with something or other when they really weren't, since I could remember what this felt like and I sorely missed it. I thought I liked earnestness—I liked it in theory, but I was bored by earnest people. But what was my duty if not to live according to the rules by which I believed the world should work, so as to do my part in bringing it about?

I was constantly aware of how easily these years of internal censure might be unraveled. I never admitted it to anyone, but the fact was that if you'd talked to me in my sleep, I would have told you it was impossible to choose between men and women. It was like choosing between land and sea. For most people there was one that was obvious—an attraction so palpable it was as though anyone who disputed it was blind. Unless you were going to be a true maverick, unless you were going to give up what good you had been blessed with, you lived on land, in the same landscape that held everyone you loved. But this was not an easy choice. Anyone who had ever been out to sea knew it could not be given up entirely. The sea was proof that the world was big, proof that it was round, proof that it was magnificent and monstrous. It was celebration, attraction, profundity. Who could go without that?

That was how it seemed to me to choose between men and women. You would, of course you would, likely make the same choice again and again. People have proclivities. But sometimes you would do something different, because otherwise you would forget you were alive. It takes a little bit of sex to remember you don't really know people when you see them on the street. Sex forces you back into awe—reveals to you just how difficult it is to know someone, just how much attention and self-delusion are required to conjure love. I thought this was how most people would live if going both ways had the same cultural ease to it as adultery. Adultery had always been treated as a kind of understood indiscretion because it allowed a monotonous life to remain bearable, gave a new shine to the things one had chosen. And I didn't want to give up one or the other—to give up the shine of life! For the shine of life, I thought, immense teams of participants were required: Men were required, women were required, respect and disrespect were required, love and the lust of hatred required.

But I knew this was not what I was supposed to want. How would I know what kinds of things were good? I had only been trained in what to avoid. No one had explained it to me very well—what mattered. My friends and I were raised without real religion and without a comparable ethics of living through which to filter our beliefs and ambitions. We had grown up with enough money to prevent us from fearing a future in which we would struggle to survive; we had apartments with windows that opened onto streets where, in our Brooklyn neighborhoods, trees and sidewalk gardens bloomed dispassionately in the warmer months. Often we did not have the jobs we dreamed about, but more often we were not quite sure what we should dream about. It was no longer defensible to build a life around acquiring money, goods, or status. We were taught to value love yet not to rely on it too heavily, because the world of excessive freedom in which we had been made would not foster the long-suffering loyalty that love required. We were encouraged to care deeply about the state of our world but our ability to affect it personally was very much in doubt. In general, we were told that the distance between desire and obligation had been closed in the preceding decades, but everyone seemed to agree that the absence of obligation would not free us. Most of all we found ourselves believing in complexity. This paradigm had some merit; it allowed us to avoid extreme states of dogma and ignorance, like militarism or participation in pyramid schemes. But it also easily justified lethargy. Looking around at the moral compromises baked into every choice, it sometimes seemed as though inertia was the least objectionable course.

I envied extraordinarily religious people, who subscribed to a code that determined the things they should want, the things that were good, and the things that were bad. They had these measures of certainty. And they had rituals that made their lives feel governed by the logic of time: baptisms, holidays, weekly ceremonies, recitations, prayers. They were, I imagined, striving toward a set of impossible ideals and yet constantly forgiven for their failure to achieve. What better way could there be to live?

To be in constant motion toward something perfect, a motion that would carry you to the end of your life?

No one I knew possessed faith and in fact religious belief was considered a capitulation: a kind of active complicity in the structures that upheld capitalism. But there had to be other ways to create the illusion of a governing logic. I admired uniforms, which signaled a singular belief in duty or in the life of the mind to the exclusion of vanity (whenever I saw Romi in scrubs I felt a surge of deference). I admired the lives of activists, who chose or found a belief that appeared unimpeachable and structured all their efforts around its requirements. But what could I possibly believe in that was unimpeachable?

Queerness rose in my life like a faith: When I came to New York I found there were shared beliefs, shared systems, not among all queer people but among a set to whom queerness meant a specific type of ethical awareness. Here was how I would know what was good to want. There was great distaste for stagnation, an emphasis on dynamism. More than anything it was crucial to learn more and more about yourself, so that you would know what to do with your body and your life: whom to love, how to love, what to fear so that you might preempt it. Among queer people self-knowledge seemed especially important because we engaged in a continuous process of recovering, of dredging up what we had suppressed, and of interrogating what we had assumed. Openness and sincerity were prized above all else under a governing practice of radical tolerance, in which speaking about anything at all could yield only benefit and in which secrets could develop only into shameful wounds.

In a life in which there are many choices and few genuine struggles, there is nevertheless no paucity of emotion, and you will find that something enters the center of your life almost against your will (though, because your life is more clearly agreeable than almost any other across space and time, the feeling that it is against your will is illusory). Something enters the center of your life. Sometimes it is a ubiquitous though painful loss, or a persistent fixation on your own inadequacy in the face of this large and agreeable life and its endless opportunities. A life knows that it needs a shape and, taking cues from films and lives it has glimpsed, chooses a core around which to bend itself. A life recognizes the theater in which its keeper appears most real.

Against all my better rationales, my life recognized sex.

3

Olivia wanted to live ecstatically. She had been going about life in the normal way—making paintings, showing up to work in her long skirts and oxfords—and this had not been enough. What I envied about Olivia was that, through Nathan, she had found a way around it.

She had been in love with him for years. Fervently, outrageously in love with him. But Nathan was that rare person exempt from love. From our first meeting he seemed to me so self-contained, so *finished,* that I couldn't imagine he would ever find himself at someone else's mercy. His resting expression was simultaneously placid and amused, his gestures unhesitating. Next to him I felt almost transparent. When I watched the way he treated Olivia I began to suspect that what he relished most was drawing out a person's emotions and desires while remaining completely untouched by them.

If he were an artist this would've made sense to me. In fact it would've seemed like the ultimate artistic coup: to be so skilled at arousing a desire as vivid as Olivia's while retaining the ability to witness it with detachment. But he was not an artist. For three years he had been leading a private family investment office in Manhattan. Once, as I was dressing to leave his apartment with my usual litany of questions about Olivia, I asked him finally, Do you mind that I always ask so many questions?

No, I enjoy that, how you absorb information, Nathan said. It's your art. My art is fucking.

—

That's not true, Olivia said to me when the three of us were together. It was the third evening I had spent with them over the course of an unusually warm December. We were at Bar Pleiades, one of a few uptown bars—complete with leather-bound cocktail menus and deferential staff—that the two of them frequented. Nathan and I were beside each other in a plush alcove, Olivia seated across a small round table.

Nathan *is* an artist, of course, Olivia said again. He paints too, you know. He used to.

Really? I said.

I used to, Nathan said.

He was a wonderful painter, Olivia said. A natural. But he never took it seriously.

Why did you stop? Did you stop?

I can't say, Nathan said.

You must not have been nearly as good as Olivia says.

He's just being short with us, Olivia said to me. He lost interest in it, because he's good at everything. Aren't you, Nathan?

Olivia laughed behind a hand. I'd noticed it was rare that she allowed camaraderie between us, and I enjoyed her laughter. Under the table I put a hand on Nathan's thigh to reassure him

I was only teasing. It always took time for me to remember that Nathan was impervious to teasing or the harder forms of criticism and that I was freed from the usual social dictates.

I thought it would require much more of me, Nathan said. I didn't feel that I could do it the way Olivia does—going home to paint after work. This kind of double life. I felt that if I was going to do it, I would have to give my life to it and live in an entirely different way. And I didn't want to.

In what kind of different way?

Devote myself, Nathan said.

And, what, I said, live on the road? Grow out your hair?

There *was* something romantic about it, Olivia said, smiling. When we were in school he lived in this sort of garret, right by Mass Ave. Yes, it was! It was a garret. His little garret. I envied it.

I don't remember you ever coming to the garret, as you're calling it, Nathan said.

I came once, Olivia said. To a party.

And you, I said to Olivia. You don't feel this way? You can go to work, come home, make your pictures? It doesn't bother you?

No, Olivia said. She ducked her head as my attention turned to her. When the two of us were talking to Nathan her face was eager, almost unguarded; as soon as I appraised her, a wariness returned. I found myself charmless and insecure. Was I blatantly uninteresting beside Nathan? Or was the thought of the sex we would have later—our evenings out were always a preamble for sex—painful or disgusting, such that she was only suffering my presence for Nathan's sake? And if so, why would she agree to such a revealing and demanding situation?

I wondered, not for the first time, whether I was being foolish and conventional in assuming this was all Nathan's idea. Hadn't Olivia approached me? And hadn't I been the one to put up those pictures? I realized I wanted it to be Nathan's idea.

No, I like painting in the off-hours, Olivia continued. She touched the ends of her hair, subdued into a long plait. Work sort of . . . fills me, she said. Feeds me. I like to be thinking about other things.

And bring them into your pieces, when you paint? I asked her.

Sort of, Olivia said. You bring everything, I think.

Liv, would you like another drink? Nathan said.

No, thank you.

All right, let's get out of here.

Immediately, a server appeared, and Nathan requested the check with an efficiency that implied natural superiority for which he need not apologize. He was flawlessly polite, and yet he moved with a swiftness that seemed, even in this small gesture, to indict everyone still loafing around in Bar Pleiades. I had never seen something quite so graceful or so alienating. I wanted to run away from him and I wanted to learn to say *thank you* in just the way he did, as though the phrase and the many people I spoke it to belonged to me.

—

How had Olivia known? She and Nathan had met in college and remained vague acquaintances during the six years since she had graduated until, at a Christmas party thrown by a mutual friend, Nathan offered her a job. He was directing the formation of a family office for a large and monied clan under the supervision of an older banker, in the hopes that the office would be youthful, innovative, and equipped to handle the needs of the family's younger generation. They didn't want their fortunes invested in arms production or pharmaceuticals anymore, or at the very least they wanted newer, more palatable investments in order to distract from the offensive ones; they liked Nathan's pedigree and his art background, though what they valued more than they realized was his firm yet gracious management style.

At the time Olivia was working, poorly, on a set of paintings for a show that was planned for late spring but that never materialized. She had a trust fund, but she was uncomfortable with leisure time or with the spectacle of leisure time, and the time that had previously been filled by her girlfriend had become, in the wake of an ugly split, time that was instead hollowed out and spiteful. And since college she had harbored inexplicable fantasies of going down on Nathan. As a senior he had made an indelible impression on her during six short months in her first year. She was obsessed with the way he made decisions, spoke to people, moved—as though he had never experienced doubt. She was a person who left coffee shops when they were too crowded or the baristas seemed disgruntled.

Nathan had said, You know what? I don't think you should put so much pressure on those paintings. I think there must be a place for you at the office. There's something about a serious job that can spark things. Challenge your ideas, create a new dynamic.

Olivia, who had herself rarely fantasized about the charms of corporate life, found that this proposed change of scene took on a surprising appeal in Nathan's voice. No, she said, are you sure? And Nathan waved his hand dismissively, as though it was already decided.

She was an obsessive person. Shy, anxious. Before Nathan she had been consumed, in high school, with a teacher who spoke too loudly and who was unafraid to critique Olivia's excellent essays. One afternoon the teacher had brought Olivia into her office and said: Do you really think this is what I am looking for from you, Olivia? Is this the kind of work you put your name to?

Now, I want to be clear—I say this because I expect a lot from you. That's right, Olivia.

Olivia thought about this teacher every week or so with a shameful wetness between her legs, and she thought of her vividly when Nathan suggested she put away her paintings and come work for him. She was convinced that there was some deficiency not in her skill set but in her ability to direct herself, and she felt at the touch of Nathan's direction an overwhelming relief and excitement. Though he had provided her permission to abandon the paintings, she found that she returned to them with fresh insight. He had never given her a sexual sign. But she perceived that his energy was inexhaustible, that his appetite was ravenous, that he was not the sort to refuse.

One night, on a work trip, she knocked on the door of his hotel room and insisted again and again that he let her suck him off. Please, please, please, please, please, she said, please please please.

Nathan found Olivia's abjection so strange, so manic—as though she were possessed, in need of medicine, or shock—that though he had never been particularly interested in her he began to approach her as he might a troubling piece of research, determined to discover the cure she required.

———

We walked up Park Avenue to Nathan's apartment on 83rd, three awkwardly abreast. As Olivia walked she looked down at her feet in their black oxfords. I had an idea that because she was an artist she should be looking at the street. Perhaps she did when she was alone. Nathan had mentioned that she took photographs too, amateur ones, just to paint from.

She grew outrageously shy as we neared the building. When

Nathan entered the lobby I held the door for her and she lowered her eyes. I was reminded briefly of Romi: She always held the door for me, always let me enter a room first.

Good evening, Nathan said to the doorman.

The elevator in Nathan's building opened directly onto his apartment. He had his own small foyer, dominated by an arresting grandfather clock. This luxury was distantly familiar to me; as a child I'd had friends who lived in vast houses, their foyers filled with fine art. But I associated this kind of money with age and vulgarity. As an adult in New York I had never encountered it other than in restaurants and magazines.

What would you like to drink? Nathan said from the living room.

Anything, I said.

I don't mind, said Olivia. I'm going to get some water.

While I untied my boots Olivia fled into a wing off the foyer that remained dark and unknown to me through all my evenings there, though I presumed it contained a kitchen. As soon as we arrived she always made some excuse to avoid the living room, where Nathan would make himself comfortable, as though she was mortified by the entire situation and unable to sit through it. In these moments I wondered how Olivia and I would ever get along without Nathan to direct the action. I remembered the push and pull I was so accustomed to feeling between myself and other women, somehow deeper than the usual negotiations social events required: Often neither of us offered to lead, and I would become overwhelmed with the responsibility of arranging whatever situation arose between us. There was anxiety as well as pleasure in the negotiation. It was nerve-racking to avoid the seat of power, to work around it or pretend we had transcended it by virtue of our queerness. These machinations had never occurred to Nathan.

Prior to this month it had been years since I'd been alone in a room with a man. As soon as Olivia disappeared my body remembered, beneath the thrill of his notice, why this was. I had no reason to think Nathan was violent, but I watched him closely nevertheless, noticing how at ease he seemed, how unlikely it was that this warmth might transform into livid insecurity.

He handed me a glass of wine. We sat on opposite ends of the couch, a worn piece upholstered in dark brocade that reminded me of furniture you might see in a reading room. In general, the furniture in Nathan's living room had a hushed quality, antiquated and almost modest—incongruous given the general majesty implied by the building and the foyer. He had green Emeralite lamps identical to those in the public library; ottomans lay at the feet of two armchairs in the corner.

How's the café? he said. You're working as a barista, right?

It's right in Olivia's neighborhood, I said, but she never comes by.

She must be embarrassed, I'm sure.

Why?

Oh, she's always embarrassed, Nathan said.

So it isn't about me?

Nathan got up and opened the leftmost of four windows that lined a long wall of the living room, then lit a cigarette from a pack on the sill. I couldn't decipher whether I actually found him attractive. He was pale, with a good jaw and a relaxed set to his shoulders. It was not his face but his suit that I always felt I was looking at, the bright-white collar unbuttoned at his throat, the way his shirt held him without reservation or pretension. He wore a modest watch with a black leather strap, and a gold ring on his right hand.

He positioned an empty wineglass beside the pack for the

ashes. I wondered if he imagined himself too bohemian or idealistic to own an ashtray.

No, he said, it's not about you. Not at all.

Why did she choose me, then?

I don't know that she chose you, Nathan said, smiling. We chose you together.

Oh? Was it you that was going through my photos?

Of course.

And you that signed Olivia's name on a message?

Can you imagine I'd write a message like that? Nathan laughed. No, she wrote that message. But we go through them together and talk about what we like. Or I tell her what I like. She enjoys that.

And sends messages for you?

It's something we're doing together, Nathan said again. One thing, among a few others. A little education.

Nathan gestured with the cigarette and I padded in my socks across the carpet to the windows. He passed me his and lit another.

But she's slept with women before, I said.

Yes, yes. Mostly women, before this.

We were talking about Olivia as though we were guardians charged with her care. Her entire affect demanded protection. Yet I was riveted by some recklessness I could see underneath it, evident in her obsession with Nathan—or, if not recklessness, some other craving that led her to its edge.

I'm attracted to her, I said. There's something fascinating about her, though to be honest she isn't my usual type. But I worry about her too.

Nathan looked at me and said, very simply, None of that's true.

What?

None of that's true, he said again. There's no need to pretend. You aren't into her. You're here for me.

I was so surprised that for a moment I just smoked and stared at him.

I hadn't even seen a photo of you when I told her I'd meet you, I said.

What has it been, Nathan said, two weeks that you've known us? A month? You go home and worry about Olivia?

Yes.

And what are you worried about?

Come on, Nathan. It's a vulnerable position she's in—the fact that you hired her, that she reports to you at work. I don't know if I believe it's all fun and games.

That's what makes the whole thing tick. That's what gets Olivia going.

Does anyone know? I mean, is there anyone she can talk to about it?

Her therapist, Nathan said. If she wants to.

The stakes are high for her.

We both have something to lose, I suppose. But you don't need to worry.

It's different for Olivia, I said. She works for you. Not that I understand what you do. What exactly is Olivia's job?

She works on charitable giving, Nathan said.

Ah, of course, charitable giving. What does that even mean?

You know what it means. You just like to pretend it's corrupt. And of course, Nathan said, taking a moment to inhale, of course it *is* corrupt, but no more so than anything else. Why shouldn't she facilitate some of the most meaningful contributions in the world? She's young, and she has the ear of powerful people. She's surprisingly good at it too, Nathan went on. She has the right attitude. Passionate, demure at the same time.

What family is it, again? That you're working for?

He smiled at me. It would have been easy to find the answer I was looking for, if I had even opened their wallets to find their last names. But Nathan never disclosed this information to me, and a part of me preferred not knowing.

This was Olivia's idea, you know, Nathan said. After she came to work for me. She wanted things to start up between us.

Still. Aren't you nervous about all the secrecy at the office? I mean—you can't keep it up forever. And I don't think she . . .

You don't like a little secrecy? A little sneaking around? You want everything to be boring and open-book?

I ashed my cigarette into the mouth of the glass.

Olivia *likes* this, Nathan said. This isn't me. I know you think I'm an asshole, but I'm not a— No, I'm serious! I'm not a sadist. This is what Olivia likes.

He smiled at me winningly, one hand tucked into the crook of his opposite elbow, cigarette floating in the other. It comforted me to speak to him this way, as though I could believe we were concerned comrades devoted to Olivia's happiness. Did I think it absolved me of some responsibility to her? What responsibility did I have to her, anyway, having known her, as Nathan pointed out, only a short time? I had always wanted to believe what people said about themselves. I figured, perhaps conveniently, that any sense that I understood people was presumptuous and immature. What did I really know about Olivia's life? What did I know about who she was when she was alone, what she wanted, who she had been before Nathan, and what she intended to be after him? What did they know about my real life, about Romi, and all the plans I had made to be a good woman?

Olivia's quite tough, Nathan said. I promise. She's resilient. She seems shy, but she's in control.

What's that? Olivia said as she finally entered the living room and sat down on the couch.

Oh, we're talking about how tough you are, Nathan said. Aren't you?

Olivia curled her feet in their opaque nylons underneath her on the couch and cradled a glass of water between her hands.

Eve thinks you don't like her, Nathan said. Because you're a bit shy.

That's not—

No! Olivia said, as though this embarrassed her even more. No, no. I like you very much. Don't I, Nathan?

She does, said Nathan. We like you very much.

———

That December I envied Olivia each time I saw her. We had met just two months after she had finally succeeded in seducing Nathan. I knew I was privy only to the most tantalizing, disquieting fringes of their relationship, but I felt as though it was unfolding in front of me. The particular richness of the experience she was undergoing, with me as witness, during those weeks—the intoxicating size and passion of it—was evident on her like a dress or a shine. Her entire life had changed in secret. It was clear she had been living quietly among all the usual anxieties and pleasures and that, when she achieved this intimacy with Nathan toward which she had schemed for most of her twenties, she found herself in a kind of fairy-tale bacchanalia: Nathan fucked her for stretches of six or eight hours, encouraged her to watch while he toyed with other women, transformed their workplace into a sexual landscape that was strange and spellbinding. For her it was love and it was deeper than the disallowed. His coffee table was littered with books, the twins of which were in her bag—books they were reading together. In the aftermath of sex I would watch them, the way they shared chocolate out of a wrapper, half dressed, first arguing, with the chiding, invulnerable ease of siblings, over which bar among Nathan's collection to choose. He was supremely experienced and it was she who not only fucked him but engaged him, she whom he found brilliant. It was as though she had turned sixteen and received all her powers at once or been inducted into a secret society she had always suspected awaited her.

This shine, its source in Nathan, was what first attracted me to him. My interest repulsed and fascinated me. He was partway into his thirties but his face was boyish and familiar: It was a face I had seen on young white men getting into cabs all over the city. He always wore a suit without a tie. The most appealing thing about him was the strength and surety of his voice, in which his charisma was obvious. He took a moment to think before answering a question and when he began he spoke very quickly, growing more emphatic as he went along. When his thought was finished his finality was evident, and I felt as though to question whatever he had said would be naïve.

Though I knew he could not arouse reverence in me as he did in Olivia, in some way his proximity excited hope. Perhaps I was more like Olivia than I imagined; perhaps I could be awoken from my life and thrust into some hedonistic way of living that would terrify and occupy me completely. Wasn't that what I had wanted from Romi too, to absorb and manifest her strength and sincerity? For days after seeing the two of them I would think over our conversations, the rhythms and details of our sex, the looks they had exchanged in my presence, the tenor with which they had wished me good night.

I should have known I was jealous the very first time we fucked: When Nathan began by kissing me—very suddenly, that was his way—I felt a victorious flush. A little drunk, inside Nathan's sprawling apartment, flanked by half-empty glasses and double copies of *Bad New Days* and *The Art Fair,* I knew that in the scheme of their intimacy I could hold them only by novelty. I felt acutely that if they liked me it would mean I was a tasteful object—the best girl in the lobby lineup. My greed was rich and greasy. Their life, as I witnessed it, was the life I felt I was owed given all the concessions I was making to heterosexuality and capitalism and the monstrous city—a life of adventure, romance, beauty, and pleasure.

That evening, as had already become routine, Nathan moved between Olivia and me as though we were neighboring islands. I felt warm and stupid under the beam of his attention. Was it impossible for us to land in this room and move beyond the bitter, enthralling drive for male desire? Olivia and I had met each other first, had liked each other, I thought. Yet the drive to impress him was so great it could not be intellectualized or dismissed through any justifications of the mind. In this hour, in Nathan's apartment, he seemed utterly capable of determining our value.

I couldn't help but be painfully, deliciously aware of him—where he looked, where he moved. While he toyed with Olivia I felt excited and urgent. I envied both of them. In moments my envy was eclipsed by self-consciousness; I didn't know how to hold my body while I was waiting for a sign that I was wanted. But I didn't wait long. During the nights the three of us had spent together, he'd never fucked Olivia in front of me. After he had kissed and disheveled her a little he turned to me, stripped me within twenty seconds, and laid me back on the couch. Once he was above me I forgot anything except the weight of him and the temperatures of my skin, the aching cool in the places that missed his touch.

Afterward I remembered it was Olivia I had wanted. Olivia I had agreed to meet, out of all the others. Why Olivia? She managed to display both innocence and an intense, willful sexuality. I wanted to study her and I wanted to put her tenderly to bed.

While I lay naked on my back on the couch she perched on its edge, still velvet-skirted and satin-cupped, only her shirt removed but her expression that of a teenager undressed in front of a lover for the first time. Her hair had unraveled from its half plait.

Are you not in the mood? I said to her finally. Looking at her I found I was bashful.

Olivia hid her face in a cloud of hair.

She's just shy, Nathan said as she moved into his arms.

Is everything okay?

Yes, absolutely, Nathan said.

Yes, Olivia said.

Would you like a smoke? Nathan asked me.

Sure, I said. Olivia?

Oh, no, she said, I don't smoke.

I'm sorry.

No, go ahead, she said. She began to pull her shirt back on. I know it's silly, it's just—I don't have a good history with it.

Oh?

So I don't smoke, Olivia said apologetically. But, please, go right ahead.

She straightened her nylons and left the room again.

No, no, I said, though I was speaking only to Nathan now.

Nathan, standing against the window in boxers, lit two cigarettes at once and said, Liv doesn't mind.

It isn't right, I said. It seems as though she doesn't like you smoking.

Even as I said this I felt how Olivia's absence gave me and

Nathan the opportunity for a small intimacy that would appease me through the rest of the evening.

She's not upset, Nathan said. She's just getting used to this.

Did I do something wrong?

No, no. She likes to watch, Nathan said as I joined him at the window.

Are you sure?

She's quite the masochist, Nathan said.

I don't think she likes me.

She's just testing things.

Though I knew that in my own way I was testing the situation just as much as Olivia was, I fumed: I was not so sure of myself, so impervious, as to be a test.

So what's going on with the two of you, I said. Come on. You aren't dating? Is that it?

We're very close, Nathan said.

Don't you think it's emotional?

Of course, Nathan said, as though I was only being silly. I adore Olivia. She's a sweet girl.

He let his left hand rest on my bare hip while he finished his cigarette. When he had stubbed it out he lounged on the couch again, moving his fingers to beckon me.

I adore Olivia, she's a sweet girl—as though she were a niece, a freshman he had deigned to fuck, an acquaintance whom he was merely charmed by. No competition. I understood that Nathan was telling the truth, but what he was saying, too, was in some way calculated to be truthful while indulging the intimacy he engineered in our hours alone, after Olivia had left the room.

Are you sure it doesn't bother her? I asked. Us sleeping together? While she's in the other room?

She likes it.

Really?

You know when you left, last weekend, I fucked her for three, four hours after that.

Nathan would always say, of Olivia, that he fucked her, never that they fucked, or that they slept together.

Oh, you actually fucked her? I said. Really? I'm starting to think that's just a story you tell.

Nathan smiled. She'll get there with you, he said.

So you fucked her . . .

And we were talking about you. You know—what you like, what it's like to fuck you, how much I like it.

While it's happening?

Yes, she loves to hear about it.

What else does she love?

Do you mean—what's Olivia's style?

She's so quiet. With me.

Nathan laughed. I would say what Liv likes is sort of . . . a fist in a velvet glove. She wants to be subdued, she wants to be dominated, but she wants it to be intensely intimate, intensely sweet.

I see why she doesn't like me.

She likes you. Just not in the way you want her to.

She won't fuck me!

Olivia likes to watch you because she likes to feel her own inadequacy, Nathan said. The painful reality of herself—how she looks.

But she's beautiful.

Nathan smiled and tilted his head, as though to say, *What can we do?*

He beckoned me again and I went to him. While he and I were alone it was as though I forgot myself, the world of women, the landscape of my life. The sex required nothing from me: I was simply submerged. I was a gift he received.

After forty-five minutes Nathan rose from the couch and

smiled at me apologetically, explaining that Olivia would expect him to fuck her to sleep. At first I felt an ungenerous pinch of disgust. It was the same feeling I might have if a friend told me she'd waited outside her ex's house all night or made a drunken scene, something so sincere and pitiful it made my heart hurt. What was being fucked to sleep, anyway? Did she require the exertion in order to be tired enough for sleep? Was she so attached to him that she would be unable to sleep outside his arms?

Then, as I watched Nathan turn toward the wing of the apartment in which Olivia must have waited for him, this struck me as a deep intimacy: that their relationship was such that Olivia would wait for him in bed, even as he lay on the couch with me. Paradoxically, given that Nathan was with me in the living room, it seemed that no one had ever cared for me in quite this way. Who had been so devoted to me that whatever their other concerns or pursuits, whatever business they owed their attention in the morning, it was my sleep and my well-being to which they turned at the end of every evening? I forgot Romi completely while I was with them: It was impossible to comprehend the existence of Nathan and Romi at once, with one sweep of my mind. What seemed in Nathan like a monumental and selfless exertion of will—the return to Olivia's bed in the early hours—would seem in Romi nothing more than baffling neglect.

———

In some way I would not admit at the time I wanted to be a home-wrecker. I believed that Nathan and Olivia's home was one that asked to be wrecked; it was too good and too ugly at the same time, too disallowed. It didn't seem possible that they were rich, attractive, successful, well dressed, well read, at home in bars that often featured lounge singers in mermaid gowns, and yet also inside such a relationship, one that appeared so private and relentless, so enviable and frightening at once.

Offered Olivia's place, I would not have taken it. Her life belonged to him. He supervised her work, determined her salary, socialized with her few friends, knew her parents. She saw hardly anyone but him, under the pretense of taking time to work on her paintings. At the office it was his guidance that determined which projects she would pursue; in private, in her studio, it was his ardor and calm that produced in her that rare creative state. This totality was the premise, the animating foundation. *Tell me you won't pay me if I don't suck your cock,* I heard Olivia say to him more than once, in the shy voice that belied her words. I was too wary of succumbing to this kind of power. Instead, in the aftermath of the excitement I felt under Nathan's eyes—and in the midst of the concern I felt for Olivia—I would contemplate how I might come into a kind of power like Nathan's, even insofar as the way he moved and spoke. But despite my wariness I was jealous of them both. I didn't want their relationship to exist outside me, not in reality. I wanted to watch it in a movie, safe from its implications or the demands of my own role, privy to all its twists and dramas.

Sometimes I stepped away from the entire situation—after all, I had only gone on a date with a girl I met online—and thought how strange it was, how cruel, that our relationship had become a kind of competition between Olivia and me. Even this was an exaggeration: I was a competitive prop, an occasional guest in their lives, nothing more. Yet the strength of Nathan's attention rewired all my desires. Olivia was now more attractive than I had initially found her, and impossibly intimidating, by virtue of her relationship with Nathan, a force I couldn't hope to rival. I found I wanted to know what it was to be her rather than to be with her, so rapt had I become at the blooming of her life.

I didn't want to desire Nathan or surrender to him, wanted instead to entertain him out of interest in Olivia. But his attention was captivating, and he was unencumbered by hesitation or angst. I wanted to believe that his control was ugly. Yet, faithlessly, I was eager for it. In the first weeks that I saw Nathan and Olivia I began to wonder if I hadn't always chafed under the pressure of leading women into love and sex, no matter how much I desired them. Wasn't there something demoralizing about it: the way romance with a woman so often asked that I advocate for myself and trust that I would be loved once I had shown how I could care for and excite her, how this kind of relationship seemed to rely on my convincing a woman of my value? What a pleasure it was to be obvious, even if what was obvious was merely my body. I knew that it haunted women that their bodies were designated for sex—even as an adolescent I had known that, had approached my body for that reason with fear as much as hope. Yet with Nathan I felt deep relief in how obvious it seemed to him that my body had a purpose, a nature, one that he could access effortlessly. Why was it that women had always been afraid of my body, as though it might catch us both off guard? In some way we had been brought up to be wary toward all women's bodies. When I was with a woman the pleasure we took in each other was inflected by old ideas about what a woman should be, and we had to learn to banish these merciless voices to make way for passion. To Nathan I was not an unpleasant reminder of his own fraught body; I did not intimidate him. He saw me and knew what to do with me.

While I was below Nathan I found that I had been exhausted by all the uncertainties of romance: by waiting, by hoping, by convincing, by attempting, even by succeeding. I knew this was

weakness, knew it was capitulation. But it felt as rich as succumbing to sleep. In the hours before I knew Nathan would
fuck me, my traitorous body would hold itself tightly, wound
up, knowing, *All you need to do is wait,* and as he finally entered
me I felt a solace so new and so satiating that I immediately
came.

4

On Christmas Eve my father called. It always took him a while to shake his pride and ask for what he wanted. We were similar that way.

I have a present for you, he said, in that too-loud voice he always used over the phone. And I thought maybe you'd want to come home for a couple of days.

Oh, I'm sorry, I can't, I said. I took shifts all week at the café.

Not tomorrow? On Christmas?

We're closed tomorrow. But I won't have time to get up there and back.

It doesn't make any sense, you working over the holidays, my father said.

Well, I have to, I said, chewing on my cuticle. I was sitting on the couch in the living room. Fatima was banging around in the kitchen making some kind of dessert. What are you doing for Christmas? I asked him. Going to Jeff's?

Yeah. But you could catch a train for the night, couldn't you? I'll be with Romi.

She doesn't have family to see?

In California, Dad, I said. Plus, she works. She has one of those jobs everybody admires. And she still has to be at the hospital over the holidays.

Well, I think she should make the effort with her folks too. But you can bring her if you have to.

That's very sweet of you, Dad.

Are you talking back to me?

No, I said. I'm just not coming. Okay? I'll visit sometime soon, this spring or something. If you want.

Would be nice if you had some paid vacation.

I guess it would. But you know, Dad, I like my job.

I know you don't like hearing it, but you've got to get a real one, he said. By next year. A job where you can take a goddamn week off. And buy yourself, you know, some quality health insurance. And a car. This whole shtick's getting pretty old, Evie.

We don't need cars here, I said.

Not my point.

Bye, Dad.

I sat there on the couch for a minute, phone in my hand. I didn't mind taking shifts over the holidays, but I hated the lie I had told—not a lie to my father but a lie to myself—that I had to work. Practically, it was true. My father was the prominent building contractor in a small, rich Massachusetts town, but he was uninterested in sharing his money with me while I remained, as he used to say in the fits of anger that preceded his weary resignation, *so goddamn lazy.* He had created his own predictable capitalist microcosm, in which I would be granted indulgence and security only once I had already reached financial stability on my own. But it was also true that I was living artificially, debt-free, in a construct of financial need. I had no doubt that in the event of true crisis my father would condescend to step in and rescue me. Hence my relative lack of savings and general disinterest in finding a secure career.

I could never quite decide which was worse: awaiting the day when I would leech off my father—as I was doing now—or attempting to prove my independence by leeching social resources that in the long term I didn't actually need, whiling away my days in some corporate marketing job. My excuse was that there was no justification for me to start accumulating wealth when I'd already benefited so much. My father was less rich than most of the other families in the town I'd grown up in but richer, by far, than most people in the country, although the narrow experience of living in this town made my father's eyes pop out of his head at the very idea that he could be described as "rich." Someday, I assumed, I would inherit some serious amount of money—I didn't know the number—not enough that I wouldn't have to work but enough that in a crisis I could step in and rescue myself. But I had none of the conventional qualities that legitimized this complacency: I wasn't an artist, I wasn't an intellectual, I didn't dream of appearing onstage. I just didn't want to rent out my mind.

That was him? Fatima said.

She stood in the doorway, licking a spoon.

He finally called? she said. What did he say?

Oh, how he wishes I was just full of ambition and daughterly love.

You do have ambitions.

I do?

Same as everyone else, Fatima said, ducking back into the kitchen. You know: Don't get too depressed, have good skin, people like you, you die surrounded by friends.

—

Throughout most of my childhood, my father was a perfectly good parent. We got along. He was grateful not to be alone, I think, and grateful that I was a quiet, easy kid.

Our years of comfortable coexistence ended when I was fifteen. He caught me in the driveway, in the dark, kissing a girl I knew from the other side of town—the childhood friend with whom I'd finally fallen in love. Throughout the winter that followed, my father liked to keep me in the kitchen after we'd finished with dinner, having what he called "discussions."

It's easier to be with women, my father told me on one of those evenings, presiding over the leftover plates and cups. His hands were open, his expression magnanimous. For women, he said. Easier to be with the same sex. I know how easy it is to have an instant intimacy with someone who's like you—to understand each other.

He took a clementine from a bowl on the kitchen table and began to peel it with his thumbnail.

Oh, yes! I know about that, he said, smiling. You see, sweetheart, love is about something much bigger than that, he said. I know you're young—okay, don't give me that—you are. Listen to me. Put your fork down. Give some thought to what I'm saying.

What are you saying?

There is something particular about love with someone who is not like you, my father said slowly. His hands forgot the fruit. The peel lay in one elegant spiral on the table. A kind of bridge, he said. You build a bridge. This is what is . . . is *spectacular* about love. That it brings you into a space with someone you wouldn't understand otherwise.

I tried to wrap my fifteen-year-old mind around this. My father had utterly inverted the conservative ideas I'd picked up about what was natural and what was unnatural and that had always struck me as evidently false. Yet by contrast, his take had some seed of truth to it that gave me pause. It was true that girls were natural to me—that I knew by instinct how to relate to them. Up until this point I had counted this naturalness as an undeniable good that would redeem me. If I chose what I experienced as natural, how could I go wrong? Suddenly I worried that in fact I was a coward, merely grasping at a true experience of life, cut off from it by my own small-mindedness.

If I didn't know better, Dad, I said, I'd think you were talking about *natural* and *unnatural*. Wouldn't I? Except you've got it all wrong. You're saying girls together is natural, it's easier, something you could just fall into like that if you're not careful.

When I was young, my father continued, I was like you, Evie. Not gay, of course. But I had all these ideas—feminist ideas. I believed in free love. In all kinds of freedom. I know you can't see it now, but men—men aren't so unlike you as you believe. They've had more than their fair share of power, granted. A shame. But things have gone in the wrong direction here, can't you see that? That feminism has warped things beyond recognition?

My father's tone was quiet and plaintive. All of the duties that were expected of us, of men, they're still there, he said finally. We're expected to be strong, to provide, to give relentlessly of ourselves, but then we've got to be emotionless. There's no quarter for our anxiety, our grief. For—you know—what that responsibility takes from us. We have . . . We respond to love, we respond to art. Could you remember that? Could you at least try to understand men, to see them as real?

My father often used this tone of lament when he talked about the loss of my heterosexual future. It was a sound from my own childhood: He had used it whenever he reminisced about his youth. As a young man he had been a very successful musician—so good that my uncles spoke about the music he had played as a teenager with a soft, mournful glow—though for reasons I never understood he had given it up. Perhaps because of the sweetness and nostalgia of this tone, I felt a swell of love for my father. Yet I chafed when he insisted on his own particular suffering. For him my coming out was another personal rejection. I was just another woman who didn't believe men had it in them to be worthy objects of love, to be more than long-suffering providers.

—

The New Year arrived and meandered. It was a brisk, merciful January. Almost a month had passed since I had last seen Nathan and Olivia, and I was all too aware that our meetings were always initiated by Nathan. I was at work, wondering whether I should send Olivia a text, when Nathan himself surprised me at the café.

But will you give me a second cup? the woman at the register was saying. Do you mind?

Not at all. I slid a second cup across the counter.

Behind her was Nathan, in a red polo and black overcoat. He was taller than I remembered. I felt an extravagant emotion when I saw him.

Oh, I said. Hello.

The woman looked up at Nathan and back to me. He smiled indulgently. I knew that smile: mannered, appropriate. It was the look he gave when I raised my hips, when I said, *You're an asshole.*

Hello, Nathan said gently to her.

The woman picked up the extra cup and wandered down toward the thermoses of milk.

Nathan, I'm at work, I said.

Nathan just smiled at me and put his phone on the counter. I had never seen him outside Manhattan. I felt a dirty flash of gratitude that Romi wasn't in the café, although there was no reason she should be—she visited only on Sundays.

I'm at work, I said again. And I know you're not used to this, but I actually work while I'm here.

That's very admirable, Nathan said. I like that.

Do you?

I do. I can see you're a very good employee.

What would you like, I said. Would you like a coffee?

An espresso. Please.

When I handed him the espresso Nathan said, Thank you. That looks lovely, thank you. Now, listen—I'm going to use the bathroom before I leave. Why don't you join me?

In the bathroom Nathan leaned against the wall beside the sink. His dress shoes were shiny with snowmelt. I waited for a moment while his face arranged itself into an expression of sincere attention. When I entered a room already occupied by Nathan there was often a brief lag like this, which gave the impression that he was deep in thought. He smiled; even in distraction he was gracious.

Listen, I said, you can't just show up where I work. I have my own life here.

Is there something you're not telling me? Nathan said, his smile widening. Somebody you have some secrets from? Is that it?

Why did you come all the way here? Doesn't Olivia want to suck you off?

I want to see your body, Nathan said. Show it to me.

I pulled my sweater over my head. The lights in the bathroom were very bright, and I knew Nathan could see my breath rushing in and out behind my ribs. He drew his eyebrows, as though the sight of me pained him. That's wonderful, he said. That's very good.

I reached for his zipper, but Nathan only held my head for a moment and kissed the warm spot beneath my jaw. My blood ran fast. It was deeply strange to see him in my real life, in the bathroom I cleaned five times every week, and just as strange to see him without his suit. Did I interest him in some way I hadn't before? Why was I elated at that pain in his brow, my breasts inches below his lowered mouth, untouched, washed out under the white lights? Simply the knowledge of that look fed me; I would have stood there in Nathan's silence all afternoon, staring past my nipples to his glistening black shoes.

—

Early on in our acquaintance, Nathan, with one hand pressed against my back and the index and middle fingers of the other circling his small pink mouth, said to me: You were made to be fucked. That's what it is.

Weren't we all?

Not like you.

—

In February I was invited to Nathan's apartment again—no drinks beforehand this time, no ceremony or pretense. Olivia stayed seated on the couch but said hello politely as Nathan let me in, and her eyes followed him across the room to the bar cart, where he was busy pouring something out for me. Her feet were tucked beneath her in navy-blue nylons, her hair plaited as usual. She wore a long-sleeved blue dress and tiny gold hoops in her ears.

I wondered how she would dress in the summer. Did she only wear one-piece swimsuits? Did she wear sandals? I could tell from the way she wound the hem of the dress between her fingers that she was uncomfortable.

I pulled off my boots and sat down on the couch opposite Olivia. My pink fingernails were garish beside her clean unpolished ones.

I'm glad to see you both again, I said.

There was no reason to fear, as I knew I would when I woke up in my own apartment the following morning, that I wouldn't be invited back; it was clear that the three of us liked one another, or at least enjoyed some ambiguous sexual chemistry. And yet I suspected that they consciously cultivated this anxiety each time we met. In the ten minutes before I left they treated me more coldly.

Things have been busy at work, Nathan said, his back to us.

Olivia and I began to talk awkwardly, with the false grace of old acquaintances meeting for the first time in years, unable to acknowledge their lack of real common ground. We touched on her job at the office and mine at the café. Nathan, she said with pride, had just completed a new ten-year plan for the family, and accordingly she had new research to conduct on the sectors in which they might have the most humanitarian impact in the coming years. Knowing that we would soon be pitted against each other—though neither Olivia nor Nathan ever acknowledged that this was what happened between us—made me stupidly cheerful and probing, as though I could try to convince Olivia, through inane conversation, that I was actually her friend.

When Nathan grew bored of this small talk he rejoined us by

the couch and began in his usual way, bending to kiss Olivia, out of nowhere, while she spoke. His swift force amazed me. Somehow it was not at all rude or hostile. He moved and immediately there was fierce excitement in the room. Our clumsiness was made bearable by Nathan's confidence. Neither Olivia nor I was ever sure how to behave. The touch of Nathan's direction, once we were undressed and at our most vulnerable, felt like a kindness. Olivia and I kissed shallowly, uncertain blood in my ears. Then she turned her mouth to Nathan's open fly.

He touched me while she went down on him. I tried to pretend to myself that Olivia was not there. It was painful for me to imagine her watching. Was this the woman I was—who would fuck Nathan in front of Olivia, knowing how she loved him, seeing how she loved him, as though her pain had no meaning? Yet what did I know about the confluence of her pain and pleasure, what she enjoyed?

After a few minutes I forgot her. I felt a mad thickness of need that always preceded the event of Nathan actually entering me. The preamble agitated me: I was nervous and ashamed of wanting attention from Nathan at Olivia's expense. But his attention held such power for me that once he began to fuck me my doubt retreated. I was only flooded and overcome. At least in the moment itself this was a keen relief. My mind scrubbed, my body filled with its special certainty.

Nathan fucked so well that I couldn't talk myself out of it: When he entered me I felt in every stroke the beast of his attention, the attention of his eyes, of his arms, of his hips, the minute ways in which, at the moment I found I wanted something, he noticed and offered it to me. I felt as though he were fluent in a language in which I was only bumbling. His gestures were no different, in reality, from the gestures of men I had slept with when I was younger. Yet he seemed to know my body by intuition. He knew the very moment at which I became disillusioned with getting fucked from behind—began to feel that it was nothing more than rhythm, with no ascension—and he moved to turn me over and press deeper. He knew when I wanted his fingers in my mouth and he knew, without any instruction, how to make me come by the weight and friction of his pelvis.

When I looked at him his face was agonized, his mouth curling with effort. Agony was the look of Nathan's desire. I couldn't tell if that look revealed his true feeling or masked it. Somewhere in myself I expected his face to be clean and smooth, as though he was simply performing his obligations.

Afterward, remembering Olivia's presence, I felt a surreal disbelief that she had observed everything—that I had been so unguarded with someone who made me so uncomfortable. Part of me relished being in the presence of a witness, yet I felt that her witnessing was quietly hostile. She sat with her feet curled beneath her on a nearby chair. On the side table lay an open notebook and two pencils.

Olivia, I said. Are those—is that a sketchbook?

I was just making some notes, Olivia said. You look very beautiful. Both of you. Together.

I got up to take a look at her sketches. Quickly she closed the book. It was strange to me that she didn't apologize or ask if I minded being captured while Nathan fucked me. Didn't I? In fact there was something I loved about it—and about Olivia's comment. Yet I was jealous of the odd self-assurance it took for her to sketch us while she watched.

We talked and it was the talk that returned us to equilibrium. We became good-natured with one another. Nathan sat below us on the floor against the frame of the couch and reached an arm up to pet Olivia's waist.

I love watching Nathan with someone else, Olivia said. With anyone.

I hardly noticed how easily she dismissed me, I was so relieved by the way she spoke about her pleasure in watching, which seemed to me genuine.

I love seeing his desire, Olivia continued, watching it play out . . .

Do you like being watched? Nathan asked me.

Yes, I said.

I always said yes when Nathan or Olivia asked me anything. I imagined that I could like being watched, even though I hated being watched by Olivia.

What it is about Nathan, Olivia said, is his *voraciousness*. Don't you think? I mean, he's good in bed—yes—but more than that I think it's just his desire.

Are you so voracious? I teased Nathan.

You don't think so? Nathan said.

Are you like this when you're at work together?

Sort of, Olivia said. I'm always so turned on at work.

Everyone must know about the two of you, I said.

They don't, Nathan said.

Absolutely not, Olivia said.

You know there are ten other women in the office I'd like to fuck, Nathan said, laughing. At least ten. Amanda. Sadia. Yes, Olivia, you know Sadia's very hot. But, he said meaningfully to me, I never would. Never. Suicide.

And none of them would fuck you, I'm sure, I said.

Olivia, Nathan said, how many women in the office?

Twenty . . . Olivia hesitated. Twenty-two, I'd guess.

And how many of them would fuck me?

Twenty-two, Olivia said.

I laughed.

You know what I want, Nathan, Olivia said. Why don't you let me watch when you have the next firing? Don't you have to fire Jackie this week?

Liv, Nathan warned.

Sometimes, Olivia said to me, the lawyers tell Nathan that he has to have a woman in the room when he fires a female employee, especially if she hasn't been with us very long—you know, just to head off the possibility of any allegations. And at first, you know, this was awful. Firing people is obviously terrible. Nathan hates it. It's so sweet, the way it makes him completely miserable. He dreads it. And while it's going on, I hate it too. People say it's worse even than a breakup—being fired. People get really upset. Or they fight it. We had a girl, when we fired her, she started talking to me, like, *Olivia, what a fucking great help you are.* It was awful.

Olivia turned one of the pencils around in her hand and started to curl a lock of hair around it. When I listened to them talk this way I felt the hair on the back of my neck stand up.

But, Olivia continued, after Nathan fires someone, I just feel the most intense release. It's amazing. So free, so clear. And it's intensely erotic, having seen him do this—so well, you know, with so much poise and determination—even though he's miserable, of course.

While I watched her I remembered, with a jolt of surprise, the book she had been holding in the bar when we first met: *Mansfield Park.* By the looks of it, a copy she'd read numerous times. There had been something probable to me then about the sight of Olivia, sober and modest as she'd seemed, with such a novel in hand—as I remembered it, a novel about judgment and redemption. There was a seriousness in her dress and way of speaking then that must have reminded me of Romi and let me imagine that she was somehow principled. Now, her stomach exposed, her eyes intent as they had never been on that odd first date in Bed-Stuy, it seemed inconceivable to me that these two versions of her were the same person. As she talked about the experience of watching Nathan fire these women she had the look of a child who has discovered something that delights them and whose only interest is in diving into it headfirst.

But it was me who was childish to assume anything about Olivia just because I'd caught her reading some novel. And, in any case, who could live according to those examples embodied by Austen's most principled characters, waiting years for that final sanctified touch, if it ever came, unerringly loyal to our ideals and our families? Despite my discomfort I was loath to say a word. Anything I might broach about decency, I thought, would be dismissed by the two of them as moralizing and naïve.

Nathan listened to all this with a small smile, his eyes on a glass of wine held against his bare lap.

Why don't you let me watch you and Olivia, I said.

At this Olivia smiled and blushed, and I felt that perhaps I had created a kind of bridge. The mood—fresh and charged—seemed to include all three of us.

I followed them down the hall to Nathan's bedroom. In the aquatic glow of the bedside lamp I could see only the unmade white bedding puckered around the duvet and a watch that Nathan had left on the nightstand. When I went to turn on the overhead light Olivia said, No, please, don't.

You know Liv prefers the dark, Nathan said.

I sat on the floor by the threshold. There was no chair and I felt it would be invasive to sit on the bed. My heart was moving fast. I would finally get to see Olivia unguarded; I was afraid to interrupt her, afraid she would change her mind. I watched as she rolled her nylons down over her knees and raised each foot in turn to tug them off. Her compact body had the beauty of a swimmer: I hadn't noticed, until she stood folded with her back to the light, the graceful solidity of her thighs. The floor was bare and my body turned cold and heavy.

Nathan was firm and fast with her. She was all acquiescence. She arranged her body beneath him with complete concentration, coiling her arms around him as though preparing to be lifted. Her voice was uneven, birdlike. While he was inside her they whispered to each other, lips in each other's ears, too quietly for me to hear. It was like watching people hold hands across a table in a restaurant. In the abstract, there was something in it that I longed for, but it belonged so obviously only to them that I couldn't imagine myself a part of it; it had none of the generic openness of pornography, likewise none of the inviting wild joy I would have expected in witnessing a real encounter. Nathan was inscrutable to me. But Olivia: The way she moved underneath him, the way she held him, told me that she loved him, that her pleasure was genuine and monumental. Suddenly, to my surprise, he slapped her face, twice.

Afterward Olivia held him with the raw need of a child. Thank you, she whispered. Thank you, Nathan, thank you.

Nathan was solicitous toward me then. He moved gently out of Olivia's arms and bent to kiss me, to remind me he had not forgotten me. While I was below him I flinched, unprovoked. I knew viscerally, as when accosted on the street by a stranger, that if he hit me I would scream.

We acted as though it had not happened. No ghost of Nathan's hand was visible on Olivia's face. I joined them and we lay expansively on the bed. Olivia's expression was serious. My fear of Nathan's slap made me even more uncertain of my instincts. Who was I to criticize consensual dynamics unfolding between adults? I was just some vanilla girl, alarmed by a moment that would have seemed merely banal if I had seen it in porn or heard about it at a party.

What is it? Nathan asked me. Are you shy?

Isn't she beautiful, Olivia said to him, looking at me. She held Nathan's waist.

I turned away from them. If Olivia and I were fucking, it would be different—desire, with its own weight—but because Nathan had positioned us as rivals for his attention, her words were almost like an accusation.

Doesn't she have a perfect body, Olivia said.

Nathan looked at me, reached out to run his hand along my side.

Don't you want to fuck her, Olivia said.

While he looked at her Nathan knelt to enter me. I sucked in my breath. A short, gaudy sound escaped him—the closest thing to a loss of restraint.

Aren't those what you want, Olivia said. Those breasts. Isn't it her that you want? Her especially?

Weren't we all? Not like you.

I began to think about how to respond to Nathan with my thighs, how to keep him from wondering what was wrong as I listened to her. It was important to me that I seem game to them, not too sheltered, not too shy, a willing playmate. *Isn't that what you like? Not me? Isn't that better than what I have?* I felt my shame writhing: Yes, I was a woman capable of delight in being measured against other women. How had she known that? Was it true of all of us? How would we love each other, then?

I tried to relax and enjoy the satisfaction she seemed to take in encouraging Nathan's momentary preference for me. But I felt I was being witnessed at my worst, in the involuntary depths of my sex, which had been borne in me over many years as a brutal reminder that the world was inside me as much as I was inside it.

Tell me how good his cock is, Olivia said to me.

I held my breath.

It's yours, isn't it, Olivia said. It belongs to you. Don't you want him for yourself? Don't you like what he's giving you?

Yes, I said.

Isn't that what you've been fantasizing about? Haven't you been lying in your bed at home, thinking about Nathan? Thinking about how much he wants you? Don't you like that he wants you more?

Yes, I said.

Don't look at me, Olivia said.

Olivia's skin was burnished with sweat, her shoulders small, her nipples almost colorless, one hand with its short clean nails flush on the bed where she propped herself up. She had such unpronounced hips that her body looked like one slim line, static. Around her head her hair was loose and turbulent, and I knew that she was wholly absorbed because she had not stroked it back. While she waited for my responses her tongue slipped between her teeth and she was still, as though holding her breath.

Fuck, Nathan said. Liv, I'm going to come, going to come inside—

No, Olivia said. Her voice lost its accusatory control, became a kind of supplication. No, Nathan, please don't.

You'd like that, Nathan said to me, his eyes on my face. For me to come inside you. Wouldn't you.

Please, Olivia said, I want—

Nathan pulled out of me and gave himself to Olivia. I closed my eyes, laid my hands on my throbbing belly. I was only a toy to them. This was what I had agreed to—nights spent as a prop with which they threw their own relationship into sharp relief. I hated and craved both of them, hated Olivia's separateness, how she evaded my touch, hated too her claim on Nathan. I had been anxious while he fucked me, and yet the loss of it was an ache. I listened to Nathan's breathing. The slap of Olivia's mouth. After he came I could hear them whispering to each other again, the words *I know* or maybe *no,* other things I couldn't make out.

While I listened I pictured Nathan's face in Olivia's hair, his hands holding her head, her body turned completely toward him as toward the sun. Why did her devotion to him disturb me so much? Olivia and I both loved women and yet we had ended up here, again and again. Hadn't we both found ourselves riveted by women's beauty and subtlety, hadn't we both relished making new worlds of our own in those private and luminous spaces that materialized when women went exploring together? Perhaps Olivia had never experienced her queerness this way; perhaps she had other language for it, which was not at odds with what she sought from Nathan. Did she want the same thing from women that she wanted from Nathan—did she feel that the dominance she savored was unfastened from gender?

Nathan had his own special charisma but his attention was polluted by arrogance, self-righteousness, moments of disdain. Before I met him I would have said his type had gone entirely out of style. Who had patience anymore for cold, educated white men in well-appointed rooms? This had to be obvious to Olivia too—she was young, not quite thirty. Yet I could not really blame her, because there was something about his genius that I coveted too. It was so convincing because his faith, like Romi's, was beyond any possibility of crisis. His knowledge and his instincts were perfectly congruent. Was his the true genius, and all our hard-won ideas about the geniuses of women only flimsy and temporary—or was it simply the appearance of genius rather than the reality of it? Was I being tricked or shown some truth deeper and older than any to which I had eagerly subscribed? How hard it was to believe Nathan was a thing made of convincing falsehoods, when his way of being looked so natural.

I had heard Nathan say more than once that his excellent taste was constituted by the ability to discern the most obvious and yet best possible versions of things. More accurately he liked the things that everyone liked, and the difference seemed to be that he got them—the most beautiful women, most coveted jobs, luxe wool coats, lucrative meetings, rare invitations. He was an arbiter of reality and value. And hadn't Olivia always expected to be used as he had intuited, if she weren't going to be thrown out—wasn't that what her body told her she deserved every morning, when she found a new rash that no cream would ameliorate, when she was shoved by the passengers she passed on the subway platform? And hadn't I always expected to be worshipped? I had tried to talk myself out of it because it was ugly, believing you were special, and I was terrified of ugliness.

You're very good to fuck, came Nathan's voice, his hand alighting on my waist. I opened my eyes. Olivia had left the room.

When I first entered you, Nathan said, do you remember? How good it was? I remember I thought of a line from Salter— this line about his cock going into her . . . *Like an iron bar into water*. Heavy like that.

I felt relief and excitement, the vast singing pleasure of being alone with him, at least for the moment. Or rather: alone with the vastness of his attention. I had an instant, incontrovertible belief in the decadence of my body, in the gift of my presence as it had fallen into Nathan's lap.

Why do you hit Olivia? I asked him.

Are you really so bourgeois? Nathan said. She likes it.

I can see that she likes it. But do *you* like it?

I'm very simple. I like intuiting what people want. I'm not interested in hurting anyone.

But you must. Hurt people. I mean, I know you and Olivia fuck plenty of people, and I'm sure you don't call all of them afterward.

Well, if you put it that way, Nathan said, I move fast, and there might be some people who have a problem with that. But I've never intentionally made anyone suffer.

I picked at my cuticles, unable to meet his eyes.

Most people I see are relatively disappointing. This isn't to say it's not fun the first time—it's always fun. But usually there's some reason not to pursue it any further. Olivia and I slept with someone recently and it was no good—she wanted to talk about everything first. She wanted to know our safeword. She wanted to know what we were willing to do and what we weren't. She said, *You must be so used to this, you must do it all the time.* And of course I went along with it. Olivia was so uncomfortable, she had to leave the room. No surprise. I just went along with it—it's too dangerous not to. But I said, *No, we don't do this, we don't have a safeword.* It completely ruined the sex. When you know from the beginning what's allowed and what isn't, what someone says they'll want, what room is there for you to figure out what's going to happen—or for her to *discover* that she wants something she didn't realize? For the sex to actually open up something?

It occurred to me that maybe they continued to see me not because I was a great fuck but because I didn't cause trouble.

What's it like when you see other girls? I said. Not the safeword stuff. Like—what do they think is going on between you?

Like it was with you, at the beginning, Nathan said. You remember. First they want to make sure everything's okay—they try to make sure it's safe. Then they want to know what the dynamic is. What kind of sex we like.

And how do you explain it to them?

I don't. They start to figure it out—that Olivia's obsessed with me.

It's silly, but I thought at first that you didn't know that. Or that you didn't want to know it.

Nathan let out a short, joyful laugh.

Where's Olivia? I said.

She's tired. I'll go to her soon.

Oh, to fuck her to sleep? I said. Can you tell me what that even means?

You want to know how I fuck her when we're alone? Nathan said. His hand moved from its idle rest on my belly down, lightly, over my thigh. Before bed she likes me to fuck her from behind, he said. Slow, deep.

His hand slipped between my legs, the tips of his fingers pressing just inside me. I felt my body turn to him.

She likes it very deep, very slow, Nathan said again. And when she starts to come, there's this halting pulse to her muscles, uneven at first, almost frantic. And then when she finally comes, it's a great clenching—one long hold where her whole body squeezes itself very tightly, her pussy squeezes itself very tightly.

Nathan began to move over me, his hand still half inside me. I let my legs fall open.

When you come, he said, it's different. That same halting pulse at first, very uneven. But then, when you come, it's an even rhythm, your pussy clenches and unclenches very quickly, like—

Nathan's cock was against me. He withdrew his hand. I felt the semi-hard head entering, the involuntary tilt—

Nathan, I said. Shouldn't you check on Olivia?

Nathan looked down at me. Yes, he said. Thank you.

While Nathan disappeared into the hall I lay in the dim, looking around. The room was hardly decorated, like a spare bedroom in a suburban home: nightstands with single lamps on each side of the bed, one neatly furnished with an alarm clock and a tube of moisturizer, the other occupied only by Nathan's watch. There was a small dresser holding a television. A door on the left opened into a private bathroom. I went exploring. In the shower were bottles of drugstore soap and a set of hair products for curly girls, which I assumed belonged to Olivia. I saw a shadow of myself in the bathroom mirror, lit by the edge of the bluish light from the bedroom. It was strange, the kind of body I became in this apartment, wide as it was and dimly lit. Anonymous, archetypal.

I thought about Olivia: Somehow she was more at home here than I was, and yet I felt constantly concerned for her. At heart I believed she was being tricked by a very good trick. It was good because it was partly real. Nathan did care for her; he was attentive, serious, electrifying in bed; his intelligence respected hers. Though his confidence made him a different kind of creature, in other respects they came from the same world. They had gone to school together; they were well paid and well traveled. But Nathan was a player in the world, an inventor of games. He made Olivia feel that life could be made up of nothing more than very rich, interesting games. In a way I could not defend I knew this was a trick. That was not the way of life. Not for people like me and Olivia. Even Olivia, in her skirts and satin bras.

Nathan entered the room again and smiled to see me naked, running my fingers over the bathroom vanity.

I think we'd better save it for next time, he said.

Is Olivia okay?

She's fine, Nathan said. Just tired. She needs some reassurance.

My worry over Olivia was quickly eclipsed by the disappointment of being dismissed for the evening. And what had he and Olivia been whispering to each other throughout the night? What had they said to each other in the next room?

I was terrified when I thought of them together, talking about me—or not talking about me. It was a feverish feeling, like running toward a door that continued to recede each time I neared it.

5

A ruthless, icy mood fell over the city. For the greater part of the winter Nathan pursued evenings alone with me. *Have fun with Nathan,* Olivia texted.
are you sure that's okay?
Absolutely.

Often we would go to hotels. My apartment's under renovation, he said, by way of apology. Oh, but I love the Standard, I would say, or, But I love the Gansevoort.

I wondered whether he was choosing to see me alone so as not to put Olivia through whatever discomfort she felt around me or perhaps to distract me from her disinterest. Equally likely was that it was simply his whim. These evenings were studies in a kind of intimacy I had never experienced outside an acknowledged love affair. Before I left to meet him I would spend hours in the bathroom, shaving and moisturizing my limbs and my pussy, plucking the hairs from my nipples and my eyebrows, rubbing cream into the reptilian skin between my toes. I chose clothes designed to convey that I was not too available—turtlenecks, oversize pants, heavy boots—and I wore all my rings. Nathan would meet me in the lobby and take me to the hotel bar. Over drinks he would tell me how things had been progressing with his projects at work: a brief he was putting together on the value projections for a few contemporary artists, a fight between two brothers over the terms of their inheritance. I found to my own shock that I wasn't bored by this. He made significantly more money, I suspected, than my father did, and it seemed clear to me that he had grown up wealthy. The family his office served included a boy who had been in Nathan's class at Phillips Exeter. The kind of money he had and handled, unlike the kind of money I had grown up around, was glamorous simply because it was paired with some measure of taste. I knew I should be disgusted by it, but I was attracted to it the way I never had been to whatever I imagined had enabled the white quasi-mansions of my hometown, with their manicured trees and circular driveways.

I avoided telling him much about my life. I didn't have to lie; I liked refusing his questions, and he liked being refused, at least at first. As far as I could help it, I never mentioned my father or Romi. Work was fair game. Sometimes he liked to ask about what I had studied or where I went with my friends on the weekends. Dependably he would ask after Fatima, whom I had described to him in one of our first meetings, and would respond to whatever I said in affectionate terms. *That's nice,* he would say with a warm smile, *I like that,* as though there was something rare and pleasurable in the simplicity of our lives. The things I would tell him were ordinary: the TV shows we watched together, the meals we shared, the dentist appointment I had escorted her to and from one Saturday morning. *That's nice, I like that,* he said. He bestowed a special grace on my life by acknowledging that it was made up of some material he was familiar with only as the stuff of stories. I felt my belonging in a tribe of women, at its deepest represented by the relentless daily intimacies between me and Fatima. It was no longer simply my minor, feminine life.

Then, as we made our way out of the bar and into the elevator, he would offer me a compliment he seemed unwilling to give in a more formal setting. *I wanted to tell you how beautiful you looked. I like you more than I want to admit.* This new performative shyness was endearing to me. He did a good job approximating the sweet inelegance of a second- or third-date confession. It was in these moments that Romi's face flashed through my mind, a sincere face from which these kinds of compliments had spilled bashfully in our first months together. I never lied explicitly about where I was on those nights when I saw Nathan, and Romi never asked about my plans. We liked living separately and were used to spending three or four nights of the week apart. But sometimes during my evenings out I would send her a tender text from the bathroom, as though I were just lying around at home, missing her.

On the first of these dates alone Nathan booked us an obscenely lavish hotel room, the likes of which I had never stayed in. This kind of luxury was so beyond my purview, even while its contours were familiar to me, that I could enjoy it without being implicated by it. Three rooms sprawled out one after another at the corner of the hotel, each graced with full floor-to-ceiling glass doors onto a deck mottled with snow. The river waited beyond two service roads lined with blanketed trucks. In the center of the bedroom rose a bath. Facing the deck there was a settee on which we lounged, incongruously, with cheap beers, a taste Nathan and I shared.

What do you think about my taking your photo? he asked me. Would you like that?

Is this something you ask a lot of girls?

No, Nathan said.

No, you've never asked to take pictures of anyone before?

Not recently, Nathan said, smiling. Sometimes. Not in a few years. It just strikes me that you'd like it. You put up those photos of yourself, didn't you?

It seemed to me that no photo Nathan could take would have anything in common with the ones I had taken myself.

Sure, I said. But why do you want to take photos now?

You'll like it, Nathan said. You're very vain.

—

When I was twelve, the central question that preoccupied all the girls at the camp I attended was whether, given the choice, you would change your face or your body. This was before most of us had real notions of what we would look like, though of course we were already painfully aware of what we *did* look like. The most beautiful among us, a blonde who had already come into a version of her figure, with very large eyes and a mouth that made her seem innocent and kind, said she would change her body. Around we went in the cabin: Most girls readily said they would change their bodies. I think it had less to do with any actual satisfaction we had with our faces and more with the idea that if our faces changed we would be unrecognizable, our personhoods altered. We would transform into cruel, orphaned girls, beautiful enough to attract the love of strangers but alien to the people who cared for us and whom we realized during this exercise we did not want to lose. (It was good that they loved us: It proved there was something more important than our faces and our bodies.) By contrast, more-beautiful bodies would only make us more charming, more sustainably lovable, easier to dress, more shameless.

When the circle came around to me I said I wouldn't change either one. I didn't want to be corrupted or confused by taking on some other shape. Besides, I was lucky: Though I looked like a child still, I was thin and agile. I wasn't vain yet, but later on the memory of what I felt then—a kind of determined self-satisfaction, the belief that I would prove myself lovable—made me wonder whether my vanity had not emerged from my body but simply found a natural home there, because the body is where vanity belongs. My body was the kind too often celebrated, white and long, somehow prim in its voluptuousness.

This refusal to participate exasperated the other girls at camp. They talked among themselves with sighs and brutal mouths, because by pretending to reject the question I had made them appear tethered to beauty in just the way they did not want to be—by choice. From the beginning I had a tendency to interrupt the rules of games, not to innovate but simply to cause trouble. It was a delicate admission we were making in that cabin—what we regretted in ourselves. Why did I have to remind them that there was a shallowness to it, a triviality to which we were offering the power of hushed voices gathered around a flashlight? It's not as if we didn't know. We knew that what we cared so much about, that what we were encouraged to care so much about and just as strenuously to reject, was, in the end, a distraction, petty, and the source of our hampering and self-defeating femininity as well as our lovability. It was stolen time, these talks in the cabin, in the full summer, alone together with no real adults around and no homework to do and the droning of the cicadas inseparable from the juicy smell of grass and the moist thresholds of each morning and dusk. Stolen time in which we could discuss what was at stake. And what I said to them was: *How ridiculous, to imagine you could change how you look, to be so susceptible to beauty and circumstance that you would want to.*

By the time I fell in love with Romi I felt madly responsible for my body, guilty and prideful. I was excruciatingly aware of the brief period of years in which I would possess this thing of unmatched value. I felt the progress of time as an almost physical pressure. On all the evenings I sat at home alone with my body, reading or watching television, I suffered from a kind of civic uselessness. I wanted to find my way into rooms where people would look at my body and say: *I see what you have there. I know what to do with it.*

In some way I was not myself until I had undressed in Nathan's living room. When I was naked I would think: *There she is, that girl I love.*

Vanity is such a sin in women, so obviously, grotesquely shameful, that when people loved my body they usually told me in a tone implying that the very acknowledgment, in any but the most tender postcoital context, was trivial and degrading. Even bolder lovers spoke to me as though anticipating I would dismiss their attention in some cloud of embarrassment. Not Nathan.

Almost every time he spoke to me I felt simultaneous relief and fear. For years I'd been getting away with this: nursing my vanity and disguising it as some kind of lofty self-respect. Pretending it was simple maturity that made me say *thank you* instead of *no, stop* when I received a compliment. But with Nathan I made no efforts to disguise myself as a lovable girl. I did not need to pretend to be modest; to him I was what I knew I was, the body I loved in its every inch, the body I could not admit to any woman. Even so, I blushed and wondered whether I should deny it.

Oh, stop, Nathan said. I love your vanity. It's very sexy.

It was exquisite to be found out. In Nathan's company it all seemed absurd and, as he put it, bourgeois—my fears of immorality, of narcissism.

He undressed me in front of the massive windows. It was warm in the hotel room. I smelled a trace of vetiver or some brisk, resonant forest scent on the hotel upholstery. Underneath my turtleneck I wore plain black underwear I had carefully prepared. While I stood against the windows he watched me from below through the eye of his phone, murmuring pleasures, directing me—asking to see my legs spread, my back arched. This was cruelly satiating as only the moment of his first entering me had been before. Here was the body I knew in private, the body I hid from women. Was I wrong about everything? Was this what my body was meant for—despite everything I had thought and believed—the routine, insistent desires of men?

How easy it was. My father, wrong again. *It's easier to be with women. Oh, yes! I know about that.* But what could be easier than this—to be valuable in terms that I experienced so deeply I could sometimes be convinced they were the true measure?

That evening Nathan was less aggressive than usual. At unexpected moments he found himself impotent and treated his cock with good-natured exasperation. This appeared to have no bearing on his confidence or the beam of his attention. At times it even seemed to me that he had forgotten about sex, caught up as he was in the careful study of my body. He had plenty to say about my clit (small), my hips (excellent), my nipples (very large), the hair I let grow in my armpits (pleasant). I found I loved this catalog. His judgments denoted an importance that I could not bestow on myself.

Do you know that you're more beautiful than other women? Nathan asked me. He cupped his jaw in his hand. I've slept with hundreds of women, he said, and you're certainly one of the most beautiful. But you would never guess it, the way you dress.

No, I said.

I'm serious, Nathan said. Do you know that you're especially beautiful?

I only smiled at him. He liked an argument. And what he liked even more was what he sometimes drew out of me—an admission of vanity that confirmed his certainties. When I was with Nathan I was compelled by him into a kind of raw state, a state of grotesque candor, in which I had unfettered access not to the knowledge I had sought out and internalized but to the beliefs that had been instilled in me against my will.

It would go like this: First he would unnerve me with his disinterested, plainspoken observations. He would say something like: Olivia does well with what she has, doesn't she? Because she's not very beautiful, beyond her hair. She has such a straight body. Like a little boy. And she's so pale. Not like you. You're Russian, aren't you?

Yes, I said, there in the hotel room. My mother's parents were Russian.

Of course, that's why you're so beautiful, because you're Russian. You have the best kind of body—a perfect body.

There can't be such a thing.

You don't really believe that. Would you trade your body for Olivia's? Or for your roommate's?

No. It's mine.

Not true. Not because it's yours. Because it's superior. When you were a teenager, didn't you envy the bodies of women who were slender, with big breasts, lush hips, long legs?

Yes, I admitted, remembering my interminable prepubescent

years and the violence with which I had hoped to become just
that kind of woman.

And do you like to be with women who have bodies as beautiful as yours?

I thought of Olivia. Our figures were different, but they
shared some crucial quality that derailed my desire for her. She
was sculptural in the way she looked—still, smooth, subtly
muscular—whereas I wanted to view myself as the sculpture,
looked at by some thoroughly human interlocutor. My fantasies
about Olivia were fantasies about the secrets she kept, her emotional reality, the journey she had undertaken so far in her life.
The hidden shapes of these were made more tantalizing by Nathan's claim to her.

Well, tell me, Nathan said. What kind of girls do you see?
Can't we talk about them?

Different kinds. I don't normally use these criteria.

You have a girlfriend, don't you? Or a boyfriend? It's a girlfriend, right? That's why you're always so guilty about seeing us.

I'm not guilty about seeing you.

No? You don't think you're a bit wrapped up in anxiety about
the whole thing?

Anxiety about Olivia, you mean.

I don't think that's what it is, Nathan said. You think there's
something fucked up about sleeping with us. That's part of why
you like it so much. Come on, spit it out. You have a girlfriend,
don't you? What's her name?

You're right, I said, smiling.

I could feel his attention narrowing in, and my own expres-
sions began to feel subtle and fascinating under his microscope.

So what's her name, then?

Romi, I said.

The name seemed to have little to do with her: It didn't con-

jure her look, her voice, the sight of her back as she pulled a
door closed.

Romi, Nathan said. And does she look like you?

No.

And you like to feel superior to her, don't you? Don't you feel
safe somehow, because you're more beautiful than her?

I smiled again, because it felt good to reveal the truth to
someone who liked me for it. The truth would make Nathan
laugh with pleasure. Yes, I said finally.

There's that vanity I like, he said, there's that girl.

Romi *is* beautiful, I said to him, as though I could redeem
myself by insisting on this. She's just not your type.

Nathan smiled indulgently.

The women I had dated were decent and principled. *I don't
believe in hierarchies,* they had said, when I asked them whether
I was more beautiful or uglier than their exes. *You'll be just as
beautiful at eighty*—when I admitted that I feared the loss of my
toned youth. *It's true that you've had plenty of privileges*—when
I berated myself for not having accomplished more. They said
what I believed and knew to be true, but they ignored our reality: that women were valuable only until their bodies expired,
that women who gave themselves only to each other relin-
quished this value altogether. It was a relief to hear Nathan acknowledge this so guilelessly. I was tired of pretending the
opposite.

Now it felt like a narcotic to hear what I knew was wrong, yet
if it were true could only mean that I was chosen. That I should
be special—momentarily and yet spectacularly special—because
I had stumbled into such a body? In my real life I saw what this
meant for women who deviated an inch from the ideal, and I
felt a miserable powerlessness so strong I could even relish the
idea of becoming an elderly person, just a house for a mind. But

with Nathan I glimpsed how easy it would be to simply relax into this ready-made achievement, as if he were saying to me, *Don't you see that what you were born with has been precious all along? That you would be a fool to disavow it?*

———

After a few hours Nathan ran a bath and sat in it with me idly.

Why do you prefer group sex? I asked him.

Always questions from you.

What don't you want to tell me?

Sometimes it really works, Nathan said. Group sex.

Not with us.

I know what you mean, he admitted. With Liv it's not immersive yet. And, you know, it's rare that a group experience is immersive, that it's really sex. Most of the time group sex is like a birthday party. That's what it is for people—a big event, a good story. Something to tell people. Very rarely it's immersive.

Nathan and I sat beside each other in a way I assumed was thoughtless on his part, our knees folded into our chests, our calves bumping. I felt humiliatingly aware of my legs where they touched his, as if it was obvious my body longed for him.

Why isn't it immersive with Olivia? I asked. Is she afraid of something? She's not attracted to me?

One time it happened to me perfectly—one time I slept with these two girls. . . . It was right after college. I was traveling. One of these girls was a friend I knew from college, I was staying with her in Marseille. She was French, her friend was from somewhere else, I don't remember. This girl I was staying with had been trying to fuck me for days—the whole time I was staying there. Her friend didn't like me, but she wanted to have a threesome, so finally it happened. I fucked this girl that I knew—it was fine, you know, she was fine. I wasn't that interested in her. The friend was watching, looking like she wasn't into it at all. It felt strange, honestly. This kind of hostility from her. Then, afterward, the girl and the friend start kissing a little, and the girl starts talking the friend into joining us. The friend has been kind of weird the whole time, but she doesn't hesitate at all. She lays down to fuck me just like that. It's weird, I can't tell what she wants, so I ask her if she wants me to fuck her, she says yes. She's soaking wet—the moment I touch her, she comes. The *moment. That's* immersive. She thought she was just watching her friend have sex, she thought she was just doing this dumb thing—going to a fucking birthday party. But then she was deep in it. She truly was.

I wonder if it's just jealousy you're talking about, I said. I came when you first fucked me.

Yes.

I was jealous of Olivia, of course.

Olivia is jealous, so jealous of you, but she enjoys it. It's such a pleasure for her, feeling jealous. A bit like the friend in Marseille. But, Nathan said, I don't think you're really jealous of anyone. You're too vain for that. But you like proof. Proof of desire, proof of sex, proof of pleasure. In part that's why I thought you might like having those pictures taken.

I rubbed my fingers together in the water.

It's a pity Olivia's so possessive about my cum, Nathan went on. She doesn't like to see me give it to anyone else. But you'd like that, I'm sure you would. Having me come inside you.

He insisted that I stay. Have breakfast with me, he said over the babble of the bath drain. Please—the breakfast is excellent.

Do you really do this? I said. Have girls stay?

No. But you smell very good, he said archly.

Once he was asleep I wondered how it was that this was the

person around whom I felt natural. He had given me my body as a perfect vessel. But Nathan's body, as he slept, was foreign and vaguely sordid. I watched his shoulders, the apparent gravity of his sleep in this uncanny hotel room. I thought of Olivia's hair come undone from its determined plait. How was it that Nathan had talked me into feeling so lucky to offer him sex, to be a woman who met his needs?

In the morning we showered together pleasantly, almost platonically, discussing the day ahead and what we might rather be doing. Nathan would go in to work; they were hiring and, he said, it was frustrating, because he found the candidates laughable. I hate talking to most people, he said, speaking through his hands as he soaped his face. Hiring people, going to functions—it's like I'm at a party with the people who wanted to hang out with me in high school but couldn't. And they're still trying to weasel their way in.

Hire me, I said.

Oh, you don't want to be a barista anymore? You have big plans?

Actually no. Scratch that. No plans at all.

Nathan grinned. You're going to make coffee forever?

Yes, I said. Don't be an asshole.

But seriously, what's the deal with you? Are you secretly an heiress or something? You wear terrible shitty clothes and you have this shitty job. But you keep up with us. You don't seem particularly fazed by—

Nathan gestured around at the hotel room, water flying from his hands.

And other people are fazed by it?

Obviously, Nathan said, scrubbing his hair with shampoo. I meet people online, and of course most of them aren't used to this. Makes things a little easier with you.

This hurt me—my sense of self was tied up in the belief that Nathan's privilege far outstripped mine—and at the same time I found myself comforted that Nathan wasn't the type who enjoyed intimidating women with shows of wealth. I hadn't realized that he preferred money to disappear. It never could, of course, and he had noticed that it occasionally disappeared between us only because I was already acquainted with it. But I found I liked him a little more for the fact that he didn't relish his own outsize resources.

I'm actually secretly a princess, I said as I rinsed the soap from my body. European. Closets full of gowns, tiaras, the whole thing. But I'm ashamed of it. Don't tell anyone.

Nathan laughed. So what will you do today?

I told him that I had the morning off; I would buy groceries, go home, daydream about how it had felt to stand against the hotel windows. Masturbate wondering what I would do about him.

What do you mean, what you'll *do about me*? Nathan asked. He handed me a towel. There's nothing to do. You'll masturbate while thinking glowingly of me.

Well, what about Olivia? I said. I mean—why is she so nervous around me? We never fuck. It's like we're obedient planets caught in the same little orbit around you.

It has nothing to do with you, Nathan said. Olivia is just very shy. She's very loyal. You're still a stranger to her.

I tried to distinguish my thoughts from Nathan's while I dressed in front of the windows. Everything was stacked against Olivia and me discovering each other, not only Nathan's influence but our whole corrupt paradigms of sex: We had been made to believe that beauty was suspect, vanity was sin, desire was predatory. We believed we were at our most attractive when shy and acquiescent toward each other.

She lives in Brooklyn, near the café, right? I asked him.
What's it like?

Yes, Nathan said as he buttoned his shirt. She lives in a very
shitty basement apartment. She's bizarrely cheap. But she has it
to herself. And her own studio.

Right, her studio. And what kind of painter is she?

Oh, she's an artist's artist, Nathan said, straightening his collar in the mirror. She's truly, at heart, a painter, nothing else. She
isn't political, she isn't an intellectual. She's a painter, that's what
she is.

But what kind of art does she make?

It's very good, Nathan said. I like it a lot.

And what does she do? The rest of the time?

She has friends, Nathan said. Well—not many. Mostly an ex-
girlfriend, this butch girl, Pam. She's very nice. Liv reads a lot.
Putters around. Goes to the park with Pam.

It was hard for me to picture Olivia leading such a prosaic
life. She was too much in thrall to Nathan. How was it that she
could just sit down with a book all weekend? I imagined her
tormented by desire for him or anxiety over what he might be
doing.

In the hotel dining room Nathan did not greet the hostess
and servers by name, but I could tell he knew them and that
they didn't mind him. He was unfailingly polite. He probably
tipped generously, even conspicuously. While I was with him he
allowed me to appropriate some part of his particular entitlement. For a while I was just a woman in an overpriced restaurant.

I watched Nathan eat a large, pretty breakfast—eggs Benedict, espresso, translucent cantaloupe and blackberries. I had no
appetite. A hearty, colorful meal like Nathan's seemed to me a

reward for a difficult journey, or at the very least something enjoyed jovially in an atmosphere of comfort and friendship. My
relationship with Nathan could not allow for a meal of this kind.
What occurred between us was not relaxed or celebratory; it did
not call for eggs Benedict or fruit. He ate quickly, with more attention for me than for the food. I only felt able to drink coffee and water. Watching him eat made me confused and tender
toward him. I wondered whether, for him, what occurred between us was relaxed and celebratory or whether it simply didn't
matter to him enough to disrupt his appetite.

—

I rode the subway home. It was good to be alone for an hour and
absolutely free. No one in the world knew where I was—
shuddering into the Canal Street stop on the southbound C
train as the hour neared eleven—not Fatima, not Romi, not my
father, not even Nathan, who always ordered a cab just before
the check came.

The best time to ride the train was in the middle of the day. It
was half empty and everyone on it had the kind of life in which
they were exempted from at least one small set of rules, whether
it was because they worked night shifts for minimum wage or
led leisured lives in opulent apartments. Or they lived by the
rules but were leaving their offices for a mere afternoon to visit
the dentist or rescue a sick child from school, experiencing with
gratitude, I imagined, the soft unpredictability of the midday
train car, the way it seemed a place out of time, hurtling along
between the real rooms in which people got older.

Across from me was a woman in what I thought was her sev-
enties, her thin hair slicked back against her skull, large clip-on

studs dragging down her earlobes. Her coat and shoes were elegant. She looked unbothered, sitting with her hands folded in her lap, her eyes moving indiscriminately over the advertisements above the seats. To her right a man squeezed a briefcase between his knees, eyes bloodshot. Teenagers swayed at the other end of the car, passing their phones to one another, as though they weren't staying long enough to sit down. Automatically I pictured Nathan seated surrounded by all this plastic, his face—as I had found it when we first met—familiar, indistinct, looking like one of the men who had invented the very rules that kept people in their offices all day.

What did I want to look like when I rode the train at forty—at seventy? Where did I want to be going? Not to an apartment like mine and Fatima's, which stank of naïveté; not one like Romi's; not one like Nathan's either, with its whiff of parody. I wanted access to Nathan's luxuries but I didn't want to own them myself. I didn't want to get cabs at ten in the morning, but I wanted to ride the train home again after a night in a fresh, blank hotel room. I wanted to spend nights here and there in hotel rooms until I died. And not hotel rooms in foreign cities, not hotel rooms where I was sleeping before I needed to be somewhere, not rooms I'd paid for, not rooms where anyone knew how to reach me. Rooms a few miles from where I lived, booked on a whim, out of desire—places where I could remember that there were always new rooms to find my way into.

When I realized this was as far as I could get toward a vision for the future, I sat up straighter in the plastic seat and felt for a moment the ominous tickle of intuition: Whatever it was I had, there was a pretty high chance I was squandering it. My small portion of beauty, my small portion of mind. Then again, I felt sure that I was drinking to the final drop from that last precious bottle, time. And what person, if they had already determined where it was they wanted to end up, could honestly say they were milking their portion of time for everything it had to give?

———

When I went to Romi's that evening I gave myself up to her in the same way, but it was not the same. How would I learn to live in concert with desire? I was thinking of what Nathan had taught me: that the only real way to fail, to fuck badly, is to know what you want and to extract it from another person.

Romi had always fucked intuitively—not with Nathan's fearlessness, but with such a degree of attention that she had learned to make me come during the first evening we spent together, years ago. Had I ever fucked this way? With such devotion that I forgot myself?

When I rose over Romi I saw the anticipatory ripple of her breath move across her stomach. What she liked best was a lone tongue. She was easy, and I regretted that I sometimes fucked her with more pride than attention. Part of me was afraid to witness a deep vulnerability in Romi, to really undo her. I think I was afraid that the power we both enjoyed—Romi's power to ruin me—would lose its heat. For years I had made her come with routine accuracy after the bulk of our sex was finished.

Now I began slowly—my lips on her belly, then across her thighs. Her body dipped away from me. She sucked in her breath, pushed her pelvis back into the bed. She laughed— a small, self-conscious laugh—then relaxed again. Her thighs were slick. Her hips jerked when I kissed her labia. I felt an intuition that evaded me when I was hijacked by obligations and good intentions. And then, as soon as her hips rose from sur-

prise into demand, my attention began to move more quickly
than I did. She brought her knees up on either side of my head
and I entered the space she had opened.

You're so good, I heard her say, the words muffled by her
thighs. She sounded shy and sincere. In her voice she was almost painfully expressive. I could hear reluctance by the way
she curtailed the end of a sentence, just by the smallest touch, or
frustration—which she was always loath to express—in the way
she hesitated very briefly in the middle of a clause. When I
looked up at her in the growing dark, even the shape of her
body seemed pure to me. When she moved, she moved deliber-
ately, without hesitation or extraneous performance. She carried her womanhood as though every part of it had a purpose
she understood completely and fulfilled with care: Her hips were
fairly narrow, so as not to get in her way, the muscles of her ab-
domen and limbs fully utilized. She treated her breasts with a
kind of resigned patience, as though awaiting the time at which
they would become useful to her. Her body made the bare mattress, the bare wall, the cool empty room with its beige carpet-
ing, look sensible: She was self-sustaining, needless of comforts.

We lay in the room in the darkness, our eyes adjusted, our
bodies planes of purple and blue. I looked down at my own
body. It was like a caricature of womanhood. What did I need
any of this for—my breasts of which I was so proud, my womb,
my wide hips? When my neglected muscles were narrow and
decaying?

Romi told me about her colleagues at the hospital, their tri-
umphs and mistakes that day. She spoke with rueful gentleness,
as though berating herself even for recalling someone else's failing. She didn't like everyone but believed that perhaps she
should, or at least that she owed it to others not to disparage
them. While she talked I smelled her two-in-one shampoo and

thought about how I couldn't possibly have everything I wanted this way, couldn't have Romi and Nathan and Olivia, couldn't have all the best and the worst things, all the irredeemable pleasures of the body and the city the way Nathan did.

Then again, why not? Maybe that was just provincial thinking, like the fear of my own vanity with which Nathan had dispensed so easily in the hotel room.

I pictured Olivia some six or ten blocks away—an unsupported guess—the window to her studio cracked to release smoke from the candles I imagined she burned in a scrupulously clean basement room.

What did you do today? Romi asked me.

I missed you, I said.

—

That winter Nathan would call me and more often than not reach me while I was waiting on a subway platform. It was like that for months: evenings with Romi that made me feel full, as if I had eaten a long and hard-earned meal in a well-built house, and then the surprise of Nathan, on the phone, appearing to pick me up in a cab or meet me in a hotel room. His voice turned me effervescent.

Why can't you meet me tonight, he would say to me. What plans do you have? Invite me along.

As I listened to him, trains I was not waiting for roared in and out of the station. I knew I would go any distance he asked of me and yet I entertained a kind of game with myself, a game in which I believed I was beyond his control. I could play with what I was in the shadow not of virtue and honor but of Nathan's extravagant indulgence and narcissism.

I can go dancing with your friends, Nathan said. Why not?

Listen—I would really, really like to see you tonight. I would *really* like to see you tonight. . . . All right—let me know.

You enjoy that I cancel plans for you, don't you?

Very much, he said. Very much.

———

When Fatima and I first moved into our apartment a few years earlier, I had taped up a quote on a piece of college-ruled paper, beside the door and above the dish where we left our keys: *Anytime I want, I can forsake this dinner party and jump into real life.* That summer we had discovered we were both tired of New York, its density and seriousness, the feeling we had that it was time we made something of ourselves. We read Eve Babitz to pretend that there was always time for that later on. It was not the sort of sentiment that we could use in conversation and we seldom talked about it. But it represented a feeling that visited me often, the sense that there was some depth I was avoiding, some sincerity or passion, a drama greater than the petty arguments and achievements that peppered my life. The moment I tried to express these things, as I am trying to do now, they became absurd. It's difficult to discuss meaning in a sincere light without the context of religion or education. I craved and feared whatever I imagined real life was. To hear Eve Babitz describe it, a cold English winter, nothing more. In this sense life in New York was very real.

Anytime I want, I can forsake this dinner party and jump into real life. Why did I imagine that what I saw between Nathan and Olivia was real life, when their world seemed so polished, their apartments so pristine, their clothes expensive, their meals unhurried? Was it just something I imagined between them because I envied their lives, or did I see glimpses of a genuine depth in the way they moved around each other, Olivia's excitement and trust, the ease with which Nathan cared for her? Nathan and Olivia were the consummate dinner party yet it seemed to me that they also had real life. The dinner party was just the setting; they were sneaking around the house, playing tricks on the hosts, stealing delicate desserts from the kitchen with their fingers, laughing and fucking in marble bathrooms.

———

What do you think is going to happen to Olivia? Fatima asked me. We were at home, in our living room. We had arrived at that point in the winter when it felt as though we never left the warmth of our apartment. And you, for that matter, she said as she filled the kettle. Do you think he's dangerous?

Not like that.

Not like what?

Not to me. But for Olivia, I don't know.

I know you worry about her, Fatima said. Olivia. About what the relationship is really like for her.

Sometimes I do.

I mean, what if something goes wrong between them? Then what's going to happen to her job, her whole career? She'd be fucked.

Listen, I wouldn't make her choices, Fati.

She could be completely trapped by him. Abused. Who knows.

I don't think she is, for what it's worth. I know it's possible. But what can I do?

You think they're in love? Fatima said. She came back to the couch and sat beside me. Do you think he'll marry her?

It wouldn't be a bad idea. They know all the same people,

they come from the same world. In fact, I said to Fatima, realizing it myself as I spoke, who better could Nathan find to spend his life with than Olivia—someone so devoted to him she doesn't care what else he does, maybe even gets off on it?

Things will probably end the way they always end, Fatima said when the kettle had finished its little crescendo and the tea had been poured. You know. The usual tragedy.

The way they always end: in tears and hiccups, panic attacks in the back seats of cabs, sleepless nights. Olivia would leave her job. For her it would not be unusual. She was intense in her emotions, which grew larger and more restless in the shade of secrecy. She would break plates and make threats on which she would never follow through.

You don't think it would end badly? Fatima said, looking at me. She had a wide, guileless gaze that seemed to hold generosity alongside the complacency that made it possible.

She wouldn't go there, I said.

It was true. Nevertheless all that winter I suffered dreams that I was on trial. When they took shape, Nathan and Olivia were absent; I was at once witness, defendant, and prosecution. If I had been called to fill any one of these roles I would have felt no surprise, knowing in the bodily hollow of instinct that I was deserving.

PART II

INTERROGATION

6

I had a threesome once, Fatima said. And I never wanted to have another one. Nothing went wrong, particularly. It's not as though I had some grand plan for it and then it failed. It happened very arbitrarily, years ago, when I was twenty or twenty-one. Remember when I was working at that brunch place out on the North Fork for the summer? It was exhausting and sort of demoralizing. We didn't make much money, since it was just brunch. But later on in the afternoons we'd be off and there would be time to go to the beach, usually, for a little while. I don't really know how it happened—I think it happened twice, or maybe it almost happened once and then the second time it actually did. Those of us who closed up the restaurant around three or four in the afternoon, me and these two other girls, would be drinking while we were cleaning up, and then we would go change into our swimsuits in the bathroom or the back of my car. I had a car that summer. These girls were bum-

ming rides from me all the time. The thing I remember surprised me about it is that we didn't start out by kissing. I think I
had noticed that there was some tension between all of us, that
there was something sexy going on, but I thought nothing would
happen, and then when it did, I didn't even realize quite what
was happening until it was already going ahead.

Why didn't you realize it?

It didn't occur to me that we could fuck without kissing. Is
that odd?

Fatima shrugged and gestured to me for a cigarette. It was the
first day of June, fresh with the promise of summer. We sat out
on the stoop. Our bare arms were pale and feverishly hot.

Well, I said, don't you think maybe you weren't expecting it
because you weren't gay?

I handed Fatima a cigarette and lit it for her.

Sure, sure. But, you know, I wasn't *not* gay. I just wasn't out
looking for it.

I made a face. The hem of Fatima's sundress moved in a mild
breeze. Oh, really? I said. That kind of gay? Like it's nothing?

I didn't think of it that way, Fatima said. It's more like I was
just interested in what would happen to me. I wasn't looking for
anything one way or another. Or even trying to figure anything
out.

So what happened?

Nothing terrible. It was just . . . very much unlike sex. Does
that make sense? Or it was sex the way you think of it when
you're a bit afraid of it in high school, or when you've watched
some porn for the first time. I think we all liked each other, but
we were very self-conscious around each other. I remember
one of the girls sounded a lot like me when she moaned—sort
of . . . you know, choked. And the other one sounded com-

pletely different than any girl I'd ever heard. She sounded just the way you would think a girl would sound. Sort of breathy, delicate, with this exquisite escalation. Every sound she made was exactly connected to something that was happening—to her touching me, or me touching her, to something clearly physical—and yet she sounded completely natural. I didn't have any doubts that she might be faking it or anything. I remember thinking, *That's just how she sounds—just perfect.* Maybe that's a way of thinking you have when you're really young—comparing yourself to people—but I thought it had to do with the fact that there were three of us, and so we weren't intimate, there wasn't really a connectedness between us. It was more like we were showing one another, *Okay, this is one way to do it, this is another way.*

That sounds kind of nice, I said. Communal.

I remember one of the girls had obviously liked it, Fatima said. The next day when we were leaving the restaurant, she was sort of eyeing us as though it might happen again—pulling on the strings of our swimsuits, that kind of thing, like she was joking but she wasn't. I think perhaps it's more about casual sex for me, or what we call casual sex, even though it didn't feel casual. It felt like this big thing between us that we were all very aware of. But by casual I mean—you know—outside of love. I've never really liked casual sex much. It feels kind of like I'm taking a test. The thing that's satisfying about it sometimes, or I used to think so, is the sense that I'm doing pretty well, that I'm capable of being this sexy, self-possessed person with no hang-ups. But doesn't that stop you from *entering* the sex as sex? You can't really get lost in it—you can't come. I can't, at least.

But isn't there something special about witnessing other people? The way that girl sounded?

Maybe I should think so, Fatima said. For example: You know how after a party, when everyone's gone home, I love to analyze how everyone acted and gossip about the way people laugh and their shoes and all that. But I couldn't really relax and enjoy it. Or maybe it's impossible for me to think of sex as just another social situation, where I'm just taking notes and learning things and having fun, because I'm so vulnerable the whole time.

But aren't you vulnerable all the time? While you're at a party? Taking notes? Feeling nervous about what you're wearing and the fact that other people are obviously going to gossip on the way home about how you laugh and your shoes?

I'm just so used to it, Fatima said.

I watched Fatima. The hairs on her arms glowed. I had been going around for years trying to figure out what sex meant to other people. Nathan had said, *That's what it is for people— a birthday party.* Special and not-special like that—a spark that means your life is happy, a show of desirability, a mark of beauty or prestige or humor. Smaller, more superficial than love. And yet I knew that the hour in which sex occurred was the least superficial thing: For that hour, at least, I was absolutely real and present, capable of feeling, intuition, care, vulnerability. Why couldn't I feel like that with the help of a little solitary tool, like meditation or exercise? Before I met Olivia and Nathan, I had imagined that I could—that all I needed to do was post my pictures online to satisfy myself and get free.

How have you been feeling about the thing you're doing? Fatima asked me. With the two of them?

After a while I said, I don't know.

Have you got anything to say about it?

You say that as though there's something to say about it. Is there something *you* want to say about it?

Fatima raised her eyebrows and looked down at the stoop for a moment. You know I don't like it, she said. How can I? I don't trust them.

I don't trust them either.

But didn't you used to be a little freaked out about men like Nathan? Fatima said.

I remembered the feeling she meant: the sense that men were alien, that if I were to foster any intimacy with a man it would be both despite and because of the fact that I could only be a body to him. And I had been right to be afraid. How can a body ever be safe when it's only a body? How can we expect that no stranger will be tempted to torch an empty house? But Nathan was not alien. He had seen the lights on in the house; he had discerned the scenes that took place away from the windows, in the secret rooms. His acknowledgment of my body had allowed me to start to forget about it. The façade of the house had been my duty, my obsession, and now I could wander away from it for days, trusting that it had proved its use.

But how could I say this to Fatima? I don't think he's going to hurt me, I said. In any case, I can't stop seeing him.

You won't, you mean. I know that when you get an idea about figuring something out—that's it. But are you sure this is about figuring something out? Or do you think it's about something else, maybe?

Like what?

Well—a desire to hurt Romi? Don't you think you're going to end up hurting her? Or do you think—maybe . . . I don't know.

What?

Fatima looked down at the stoop again. I'm sorry, she said. But don't you think you might be addicted to sex?

Really? Aside from this, all I've been doing is having sex with

Romi a few times a week. For years. Do you really think I go looking for sex that often? Like it's dangerous?

What do you think this thing with Nathan is, Fatima said, if not dangerous?

I come home safe every time, don't I?

There's no guarantee. You've said it yourself.

Fati—

We might as well take a survey. Just to think it through. Couldn't hurt.

All right, I said.

And what about Romi? You're not telling her, I assume?

No. I'm not telling her. Obviously.

Aren't you worried about her finding out?

This had hardly occurred to me. My fear was not that Romi would find out but rather that she would trust me endlessly and that I would only sink deeper into ignobility, comparing myself to her and hating my own nature. Fatima saw my face and frowned.

How does it feel? she said. Lying to her?

I don't know.

Don't you feel bad?

Yes, I said. I feel bad when I remember it—that I'm lying to her. But most of the time it feels good. Not just Nathan but the two things. Having both. I feel so free. I have this feeling like I can go anywhere I want, do anything I want. Have anything I need.

You know that you can have that without lying, Fatima said. You can just be with people who are down with it, with being open, polyamory, whatever. Or ask Romi—who knows?

I knew that in theory Fatima was right. Yet so much of what I envied in Nathan was not just his freedom but his ease with secrecy. It was one thing to move between people who loved you with absolute transparency, knowing what you owed each of them, knowing what they expected of you. It was another to move between people who excited you while you hid that whole private carnival of your life. I had seldom felt such rich, exultant freedom as I did harboring this secret that mattered to no one but me. I remembered suddenly the exhilaration I had felt, hiding in Romi's bathroom, as I watched Olivia respond to my first messages in real time.

—

It wasn't true that most of the time I felt good, as I had told Fatima. I moved between high and low emotions with speed. If I couldn't live ecstatically, at least I could live at this fever pitch, which on the best days allowed for ecstasy. What felt good was that my life was newly vast. I still lived in little dark rooms, but I was no longer bounded by the old parameters. I was moving through scenes and sets without compromise. There was time for Romi, time for Nathan and Olivia, time for work and play. When someone asked how I was I no longer told the truth; instead I luxuriated in the knowledge that the truth about my life was protected, kept safe from the pollution of salacious interest or the moral anxieties of others.

There was only so much I could hide from Fatima. She heard me enter and leave the apartment at odd hours, heard me when I spoke on the phone, heard me when I cried. Around her I felt most acutely the wrong I was doing to Romi.

Why *was* I doing this to Romi, when I loved her with such gratitude? Why was I so eager to trouble the future between us? Why was it so difficult for me to believe that women could be inevitable, that sooner or later we would end up together, the way men believed that of me? There had been years that it was fun to laugh at men who were so certain of themselves. But now there was nothing amusing in it for me, nothing ridiculous about it. Thank you, Nathan said each time he handed the cocktail menu back to the server, and there was no trace of apology in his voice. He was not trespassing; nowhere he went did he trespass, and it had never occurred to anyone to question him. Thank you, I said to his doorman on the way out of the building, late in the evenings, but each time it was an apology.

—

Romi, too, had a doorman, who had grown used to seeing my solicitous look in the lobby and nodding toward the elevator in response—permission granted. Romi's spare key lived under a doormat, like everyone else's. I envied her unthinking trust in strangers. On the days when I worked the morning shift and got off in midafternoon, I liked to let myself in and hang out in her empty apartment until she finally finished work.

I knew every corner of her place. There were no secrets to find. Her drawers were half empty, her carpets regularly cleaned by the building's staff. She kept a fresh store of things I liked to eat in the fridge: bowls of pomegranate seeds, soft cheeses. Every object in the kitchen, in the closet, in the bathroom, had a purpose. Sometimes I would put on a pair of Romi's scrubs and marvel at how easily I too could be transformed into a purposeful object. Looking down at my formless pale-blue body, I felt poised and trusting, sure that I had the resources to solve any problem that might come my way.

When Romi came home one evening to find me lying on her bed wearing her scrubs, holding a book over my head, she smiled the way I imagined she smiled at her patients.

You like how those look, baby? she said, putting down her bag in the doorway. She did a little spin. She was still wearing her own scrubs. You want to match?

They're so comfortable, I said.

They are, she said. But I think you'd get sick of them.

We ordered takeout and Romi insisted she would go to pick it up. I could use the exercise, she said.

While we were unpacking the plastic containers and arranging them on the coffee table, I asked her whether she had ever considered men as an adult, after the confusion of adolescence had resolved itself.

Oh, sure, she said. You know—sort of idly. Just thinking about it. What men are like. Whether I'd want to touch one.

And?

I would. I mean, just to sort of see what it's like. She sat cross-legged on the floor beside me and punched a plastic fork through its envelope. And to sort of watch that kind of thing, she continued, thinking, her eyes moving over the ceiling. A man's libido. How it feels. But it isn't desire, it's just curiosity. I don't actually want to fuck them.

She took the plastic tops off the takeout containers. Then she licked her thumb and looked at me curiously.

But weren't you ever tired of all the uncertainty? I said.

Romi laughed.

I'm serious, I said. There's this thing, when you're girls, where you circle each other, wondering what the other is thinking, wondering who will make the first move, what it means to make the first move, what it means to *want* something as a woman, let alone to want another girl. At one point I just thought it was so tiring. I wanted to be sure of something. Sure that someone wanted me.

That was what happened with that guy from Amherst? Romi asked. In college?

Didn't you ever struggle with that? I said. The part where everything is all muddled?

Romi handed me a stack of napkins. Yes, she said. I was always very shy, and everything—any kind of romance—always felt very uncertain to me. It's always hard to know what's going on between me and a woman. Even between us, you remember, it took us a while to . . .

Yeah, I said, and touched Romi's leg, bare below her running shorts.

But I'm grateful for that, at least when I have the wherewithal to be, Romi said. I mean, who wants to just slot into the role they've been told to slot into, make no fuss, roll along with it, just marry some guy and fuck him like you were brought up to?

Romi! I don't think I've ever heard you be so vulgar.

Is it vulgar? she said. I mean, weren't we brought up to fuck men, even if no one wanted to admit that was what was happening?

Of course.

And once things get going, you know, between women, Romi said, it's so much more intense because of that. Because it was so uncertain.

You mean the way there isn't a script, that you have to make it up between yourselves as you go along? *How did you know? Weren't you scared?*

Romi kissed me. Like that, she said.

I watched her while she began to eat. When I was first falling in love with her, I'd had the sense that beneath her unassuming jogging clothes and the shell of her apartment, Romi resembled a literary hero: a man out of Austen, like Darcy, or *Mansfield Park*'s Edmund Bertram. She had that religious social sense, that uncompromising sincerity. She'd shown the willingness, in her last relationship, to endure a long and harrowing love. I had no doubt that if the need arose she would rescue some cousin of mine from a tough spot, never implying where credit was due at a family holiday. She was kindhearted and generous—why should she ever feel uncertain? If she was capable of wrong-doing, she was unaware of it. Perhaps it was this blindness that enabled her generosity. Did she ever really pay attention to her feelings, think about them, worry about them? She paid attention to the needs of other people and the world. When she wanted something, she told herself it was good to have what she wanted. Her affect was robust and decisive.

I was arranging a plate of noodles and dumplings when my phone rang.

It's my father, I said. One second.

I got up and walked the few yards to Romi's bedroom.

Evie, it's been a while, my father said when I picked up. It's been months. And you haven't come to visit.

How are you? I said. What've you been doing?

Oh, this and that. Working, you know. Always working.

I closed the door and leaned against it. The carpet here was worn away by the motion of the door.

That's good, I said. Good.

What about you? Applying to jobs, I hope?

Oh, yes, I lied. Yeah. When I see them.

Really?

Yeah. Romi's helping me.

What does she know?

She has a great job, Dad, remember?

Well, you don't have a medical degree.

That's true.

You have, pardon my French, an absolute shit degree. A waste, Evie. Don't you think?

His tone reminded me of an evening not long after Romi and I had started dating, when I first brought her home for Thanksgiving. My father was gruff and a little awkward, as usual, but beyond the idea that Romi and I were together, he liked her, as I had expected he would. We helped him cook the side dishes: creamed spinach, sweet potatoes. When we finally sat down to dinner he was gratified to hear about Romi's upbringing—her parents were also doctors, still married—and about her medical training and volunteering.

Why don't you train as an EMT too, hmm? he said to me that evening, gesturing with his fork. You don't need to be a doctor.

I don't want to steal Romi's spotlight, I said. Besides, I have plenty to do.

She calls that work, he said to Romi, with a conspiratorial smile. What do you think? Would you call that work? Making coffee on a machine?

Romi met his eyes in that admirable way she had. She was the sort of person who volunteered to run anonymous question sessions about sexual orientation at work or to send campaign texts to registered Republicans with some bipartisan appeal.

I certainly think so, she said. I see how hard Eve works.

But what is she really *doing*? my father said. It just disappears! Poof! You make the coffee, they drink it, suddenly you're old.

I can imagine, building houses, how important it is to you, Romi said. To make something that lasts.

Well, of course, it's important to all of us. To have something to show for your work. And there's nothing there for you, Evie, nothing in that spot. No fruits of your work.

Instead of harassing my father about our differences I had begun, years ago, to practice what I believed was forgiveness by trying to act as though I was impervious to his disdain or his disappointment. Over time this imperviousness was hard to distinguish from silence. My father couldn't imagine that any action on his part had provoked or encouraged my reticence. He accused me of distraction and carelessness. Nevertheless he would call every few months, since after all I was his only child, we were each other's family, the little family we had left, why weren't we more loving toward each other, why couldn't I see he only wanted me to be happy?

After a beat I said into the phone, I guess that's why I'm not having any luck finding a job. Just my stupid degree. Are you calling about something?

Listen, he said. I'm calling, actually, because you know your birthday's coming up.

Yes.

Well, I wanted to get you something.

Oh, I don't need anything.

Jesus, Evie, my father said. His voice rose. All right, you don't need anything, you don't want anything, clearly, or you'd be making it happen for your goddamn self, wouldn't you?

I'm not trying to be—I don't mean it that way, I said. I just can't think of anything I need, that's all. And you know I don't have much space.

Because you're living in what is essentially a dorm room, you mean.

Sure.

Why don't we make a deal, he said. I want to get you something special, but we'll save it until you get that job. A real one. That way it'll be a proper celebration. Since I suppose there's no reason to reward you for getting any older.

No reason, I said.

How old is it this year? Twenty-eight, twenty-nine?

Twenty-eight.

No reason to reward you for making it all the way to twenty-eight and earning, what, twenty grand a year? he said. With everything I gave you?

Everything he had given me: a litany about which we were both ashamed, in our own ways. Ballet lessons, a math tutor, money for school trips. I hadn't gone to Exeter, I hadn't developed Nathan's immense certainty, but I was plenty selfish.

Bye, Dad.

I went back into the living room and put my hand on Romi's shoulder.

What was it? she said. Is he okay?

He's fine, I said. The usual.

Romi gave me a gentle look. I'm sorry, she said. He's not happy?

What I really wish, I said, feeling the small soft hairs at the back of her neck, is that he would just be proud of *you* for once. I mean, I'm fine being a disappointment. Have been for a long time. But you? Romi? The doctor?

Stop, Romi said, with the look of bashful gratitude that happy people use when their happiness is deserved.

While Romi was cleaning up I saw I had two messages. From my father, a link, the headline preview of which read: *Twelve Tips on Taking Advantage of Your Twenties*. From Nathan, I had a short, rare message: *I've been thinking about you.*

———

Later that week I met Nathan and Olivia for dinner out in Clinton Hill. The invitation surprised me. I hadn't seen Olivia since our midwinter meetings in Nathan's apartment uptown.

Nathan chose a small Italian restaurant I had been to once before, with Fatima. It was unobtrusively tucked inside an old storefront. I arrived earlier than I intended, but I didn't want to show that I was eager or be found awkwardly waiting at a bar. Instead I smoked and walked four times around the block.

When we sat down Olivia began to do her cursory check around the restaurant: Who was there? Was there anyone they knew?

Relax, Nathan said. We're in Brooklyn.

And you're just having dinner with a friend, I said. Right?

Of course, Nathan said.

It was hard for me to recall the rush of determination I had felt toward Olivia when we first met the previous December. I had spent too much time feeling, in turns, rejected or used by her, when I was not sunk in anxiety about the defensibility of my *own* conduct. But she continued to fascinate me. I felt toward her now the way one might toward a celebrity—intensely curious, distant, and admiring, yet without any hope of reciprocal interest.

Olivia, I'm so glad to see you, I said. How have you been? Why haven't I seen you?

Oh . . . She blushed. I don't know. I've been very busy.

Busy?

Yes.

Have you been painting?

Olivia looked down at her empty plate. I suspected that she had warmed to the idea of me after a period of unwillingness, or perhaps been talked into another attempt. Wariness hung over my body, which had become, in the preceding months with Nathan, accustomed to languor.

After we ordered we asked each other the requisite questions about work.

Nathan showed me some pictures of your paintings, I said to Olivia. Some of the more recent ones, I think? They're wonderful, Olivia.

Nathan and Olivia exchanged glances in the natural hush that fell while the first dishes arrived. Olivia began to disassemble a cauliflower tart with her fork.

This is really good, she said to Nathan. You'll like it.

Really, I said to Olivia. I'm happy I got to see a little of it.

Do you want some of this? Olivia said to Nathan.

Olivia, I said. I'm only trying to compliment you.

Olivia ignored me. I watched while the two of them played a game, Olivia insisting on serving him from her fork, almost maternally, and Nathan in turn protesting, acquiescing, smiling. I was embarrassed for her and jealous at the same time. Finally Nathan turned to me with a little amused look, as though to thank me for indulging her.

They're beautiful, I said again to Olivia.

Olivia was still toying with Nathan's plate. Oh, just stop it, she said finally.

Nathan, I said, help me out here. Anytime I want to talk to Olivia about her work, it's like I don't exist. Will you help me? Can you get her to talk to me a little?

Nathan, Olivia said, are you too crowded under there? Should we try to get a different table?

Our table was situated in the middle of the cramped restaurant, our knees doing battle beneath the paper tablecloth. I liked the little conspiracy of Nathan's knees and I liked not worrying while Olivia worried.

Nathan laughed. Liv, he said, why don't you want to talk about the paintings?

You know, I said to Nathan, I even sent Olivia some messages, to tell her how much I liked the work! I mean, I was moved by it. I was really excited to see it. And she didn't respond, not at all. She never responds to me.

Really? Nathan said. Olivia, you don't respond?

She never responds, I said.

Olivia ignored us both and began to eat the tart. I refilled our water glasses from the carafe so I wouldn't be forced to stare at her. How had I stooped to this: *Can you get Olivia to talk to me?*

In my gut I felt it as a betrayal, not so much of Olivia as of myself, the way I knew, when I got a job or a letter or an introduction from a man, that I had done it with my smile and a flirtatious set of my shoulders, though my friends and I would pretend to one another that I had done it through will and intelligence. We were just having dinner, I told myself, I was just teasing, trying to penetrate Olivia's shell. But in truth I was succumbing to the apparatus in which Olivia and I lived—susceptible to Nathan's lightest touch—while Olivia, who was normally so seamlessly acquiescent to Nathan, grew red-faced and galled in her attempt to resist it. Clearly she was loyal to her work even at Nathan's expense. Here it was, the thing that she would not compromise.

Liv, Nathan said.

Olivia laid her fork down on her plate. A sharp, cold sound.

I don't want to talk about this, Olivia said. I won't talk about this.

Why not?

I absolutely won't, Olivia said. I won't discuss this with you. I don't want to talk to you about my work. I didn't want to show it to you. I don't want it to have anything to do with you. It's private. And the thing that makes me absolutely livid, she said, her eyes wide, her mouth set, the thing that makes me absolutely livid is the fact that you think you get to be a part of my work, that you deserve a response from me. That you can look at my work and ask me about it, expect me to respond when you bring it up with me. Like it has something to do with you.

I was flooded with shame.

I'm sorry, I said. I'm sorry, Olivia.

Nathan was amused. He liked to see Olivia angry. Even as it surfaced in the restaurant her upset had a sexual color. Olivia, he said, she's just being nice. She just wants to be friends with you.

Yes, I said—humiliated by this kindness.

And besides, Nathan said, everyone's going to see the work. Everyone's going to be talking to you about it, asking you about it. It isn't private, not anymore. It's going to be a big deal. Liv has a new gallerist, he added to me.

While I listened to Nathan talk I thought: What I kept for myself I kept selfishly, without some noble artistic agenda. I could never defend myself the way Olivia had. Sometimes it disgraced me to behold her. It seemed that she was wild where I was repressed, that she had an unmatched capacity for life, that what I called joy or anger was merely a shadow of what she felt.

Olivia was embarrassed again. I'm sorry, she said. I'm sorry, I didn't mean—I just don't want to discuss this with either of you. I don't want to talk about my work. Excuse me.

She got up, ostensibly to use the bathroom. Nathan smiled encouragingly at me.

She isn't really angry, he said.

Nathan, I said, you're full of shit. She is obviously angry.

No, she isn't. She'll get over it.

She *is*! She will get over it, sure. But she's definitely angry. I upset her.

I know Olivia much better than you do, Nathan said.

I don't think you understand *this*. This, Nathan, about her work. It's a serious thing for her. You don't understand this part the way you think you do. We shouldn't be pushy about it.

She'll get over it, Nathan said again. This is good, don't you think? This cauliflower.

I ate the cauliflower and wondered how it was that Olivia had it in her to say, *What makes me absolutely livid is the fact that you think you deserve a response from me.* When had it ever occurred to me, when I heard someone compliment me, to feel anything but gratitude and the obligation entailed by gratitude? After all this time trying to understand if there was anything that belonged to Olivia alone, any kernel of herself she protected even from Nathan: At the moment at which I discovered it, I had no respect for it. I wanted her to surrender her privacy completely.

I apologized to Olivia again when she returned to the table. Nathan did his part making peace between us. But I felt that I had gone too far, seen the limits of Olivia's obligatory kindness, and seen, too, the proof that it was obligatory. She tolerated me for Nathan's sake and would not allow a person she merely tolerated into the realm of her private work. As usual Nathan offered me something seductive and, inevitably, false: that sense of my own entitlement.

While we waited for the check Nathan doodled on the paper tablecloth, signing his name over and over in efficient script. This was at once embarrassing and endearing to me. I felt sud-

denly as though I really knew him—not only that, but as though
he was more real than other people I felt I knew. He unselfcon-
sciously confirmed an ugliness I had witnessed in myself and
others, witnessed and attempted to deny.

Olivia gave me a furtive smile. A peace offering.

Isn't that awful, she said. How childish he is? Do you see what
he's writing, over and over?

I do, I said gratefully. I'm not surprised.

Nathan smiled and continued running his pen over the tablecloth.

Sometimes, Olivia said to me, her speech halting and
thoughtful, it's refreshing to be with you. Because, you know,
I'm so enamored with Nathan that I can forget how absurd he
is! How arrogant. I don't notice it at all. I mean, I do, but I enjoy
it. All of it. You know—I'll be on the phone with him while he's
just going around, doing his things. Getting coffee or buying
things . . . I don't know. And I'll hear people being so nice to him
on the other end, being so *charming,* just flirting with him, asking him things—I can tell they're smiling!

Baristas, Nathan said. Baristas love me.

They do, Olivia said. He tips well. And he's very charming.

You know just how charming baristas find me, Nathan said.

Olivia found her umbrella beneath the little table and
whacked Nathan's arm lightly. She was easygoing again. While
we walked out onto the street I relished the thought that my
company forced Olivia into some reckoning with the grotesque
reality of Nathan. Yet hadn't I taken Nathan in pleasurable stride
all evening? *You're full of shit,* I'd said, but we had been—in my
mind, in the war I had created—on the same side. I suspected I
had refilled his water glass three times. Nathan's company lulled
me more deeply than ever. When he disgusted me it was not a

disappointment; every turn in his personality had a place in my geography of relationship, felt fertile.

———

We went to Olivia's apartment. It was a small, spare basement studio, carefully decorated in an old-fashioned style, with a heavy wooden desk painted red and two vases of cut flowers on the slender kitchen table. Despite the pleasant life I shared with Fatima, I felt as though I were entering a dream I'd once had, a dream about being a woman living alone among beautiful objects. The trees just visible outside Olivia's window glowed green. She and Nathan were outlined by the bedside lamp, against the varnished wood and the navy bedspread.

Nathan wanted to fuck us together, perhaps because he understood that we needed uniting and wouldn't manage it alone, or perhaps because he knew jealousy would divide us further. Time and again I failed to understand.

He fucked Olivia first. Before he began he said to her:

You have to kiss Eve if you want me to fuck you. Don't stop, or I'll leave.

I kissed Olivia as he implied that I should. I liked lying close against her underneath Nathan's arm, feeling a part of their couple.

Olivia tested him. She breathed or pulled away from me to hold him, but he withdrew.

Kiss her, Nathan said. Or don't you want me to fuck you?

Olivia kissed me shyly. When the three of us had established a rhythm, steady kisses, his cock moving faster, she broke from my face to say, Nathan! Thank you, thank you, thank you!

For a moment I shut my eyes and turned away from her—

I couldn't bear to look at her while she thanked him, her child's eyes, the long expanse of her throat as she arched, the nakedness in her face. Nathan's expression was brutally focused, as though at any moment he might finally break the door from its hinges. *Thank you, thank you*—God, had I ever let that slip, when I was underneath Nathan? Had I even thought it?

When he turned to fuck me he gave the same instructions. Olivia kissed me in her closemouthed way. Slowly, inside Nathan's embrace, I was happy, sweet, ecstatic again, I loved being between them, I loved being one with them. The air in the room grew thick with our breath. We escalated in tandem. I wondered if this was the heart of what I had always looked for—multiplicity, communion, a desire richer and larger than any singular desire, each of our wants absorbing the others and growing into a new kind of animal, ravenous and herculean. My own desire was blameless, swallowed up by the scene.

It was over before I was ready—a small heartbreak—my body still hungry.

Nathan pulled out of me and lay beside me on Olivia's bed. I rested my hands on my belly, as I did in sleep. Nathan held the first two fingers of my right hand in his fist while he touched himself with the other. My fingers in his hand were gripped completely. They grew warm while my breath returned. I felt myself poured into those fingers as though I could remain so surrounded and warmed. How could it be this that I wanted? Muted, held, warm, told what I was. By a man like him.

Olivia put her mouth on Nathan's cock. I was grateful that she loved going down on him; it was a kind of subjugation that I had always disliked. I could imagine enjoying it, perhaps, by feeling as though it filled me with a particular kind of power— the ability to manipulate the pleasure and increasing helplessness of a person. Fatima had said she felt this way sometimes.

But the way Olivia sucked him had nothing to do with this. Her love was obvious in everything she did for him, yet here she was even more consumed by feeling. There was none of the calm passivity that overcame her when he fucked her. She was rhythmic, focused, energetic. She was moved by going down on him; she moaned and moved her hips in involuntary starts. Watching her I wondered whether it was the act that mattered most to her: It was abjection itself, becoming completely, and with ardor, the anonymous hole. *Sometimes I like him to be on his phone while I go down on him at the office,* I remembered Olivia had said some other evening, when our cocktail conversation had shifted into sexual play, *so I can feel like he isn't paying attention to me at all.* Olivia was willing to follow him, to go all the way down. No part of her was appalled. She was unencumbered by rhetoric, unencumbered by belief. Was she never divided, not even for a moment, between the parts of herself that she loved and the parts that scared her? What was it that appalled her mind that her body could not refuse?

Nathan took a long time to come and when he did Olivia was more delighted than he was. He lay with his hands over his face, Olivia's sheets soaked in his sweat. She laughed when she felt the bedding. Then she put on a long black shirt and went to the kitchen in the corner of the room.

What would you like? she asked Nathan. Water? Sauternes?

This was a wine Nathan liked and often ordered at restaurants.

Nathan didn't answer.

Olivia, I said, where's your studio?

Oh, it's through there, she said, gesturing at a small door adjacent to the basement's half windows onto the street. I had taken it as a closet. There were no pictures up in her apartment, neither hers nor anyone's—only the purple hydrangeas on the table, and various vases that looked as though they had been acquired at the proliferating Brooklyn specialty stores stocked with ceramics and delicate leather goods. Stacks of paperbacks overflowed from two bookcases lining the wall.

Nathan, what would you like? Olivia said again.

Do you like watching Olivia go down on me? Nathan asked me.

Yes, I said.

Olivia stood in the center of the room, observing us.

Do you think I look like a whore when I do it? she said.

I thought for a moment about saying yes, because I tried to say yes to every question they asked. I guessed that she wanted to be perceived this way because the world into which Nathan had brought her—sleeping with him, sleeping with me and other women—made her promiscuous in contrast to her past. She wanted to revel in that newness.

Rhetorical question, or real? I said.

Olivia looked at Nathan.

Real, Nathan said. Of course.

No, I said. You never do. Do you mind my saying so?

It's because my tits aren't big enough, Olivia said, with a dejection that made me laugh.

No.

Why not, then?

You're so devoted to Nathan, I said. Forgive me. But it's obvious that you love him, when you do it.

That's true, Olivia said.

Nathan gave me a generous smile, the same smile he gave when I told him about the intimate routines Fatima and I shared. He turned the ring on his right hand idly. Then he closed his eyes. That's nice, he said. That's very nice.

Olivia's love was something very nice, like an unexpectedly

good meal or a strong day for Wall Street. It pleased him in passing but it didn't penetrate his inner life, the place where he understood himself and contrived plans. I had assumed, in the beginning, that he must be blinded to the size of her love by proximity, or that, if he understood it, he was callously uninterested in her well-being. But he was neither. Both of them understood what was between them very clearly: Olivia loved him in part for this balance of which he was distinctly capable; she enjoyed his ability to indulge and deepen the degree to which she had fallen for him without demanding anything from her. His self-reliance was part of his appeal, to her as much as to me. I still thought sometimes it must pain her, how indebted she was to a feeling to which he was immune. I knew she was afraid of his leaving her. But I had underestimated her, that was also true. I had thought that, despite her intelligence, she was somewhat delusional.

The more I understood this the more I envied Nathan. If he wasn't cruel, then I had no cause to hate him, only to envy him. I wondered how I could get what he had—absolute freedom, a life of embodied prowess, in which I might float through a landscape of love and sex without promising myself to anyone.

Nathan, what would you like to drink? Olivia asked him again.

I think maybe he's asleep, I joked.

Olivia sat beside Nathan and rolled a clementine against the skin of his forearm. Maybe all my justifying was in vain and she was on the railway platform—waiting endlessly for the decisive arrival of answered love. I saw her there, the evening growing cold, her hair half tucked into her coat collar, leaning slightly over the platform at the phantom light approaching. The openness in her face made me feel absolutely sweet toward her. Who in the world could be a better friend to her than I could, when only I knew how she spent her nights, knew how she felt?

Olivia, I said.

I felt a surprising boldness. Olivia gave me a small smile. When I kissed her she returned it softly, in her chaste way. The clementine rolled out of her hand onto the bed. She leaned forward with her whole body, then leaned away once the kiss had been bestowed. I thought she was enjoying withholding from me a little. I moved my fingers over her back. Cautious, tender. She closed her eyes—in shyness, in pleasure?—my palm on her waist, lifting her shirt. She smelled clean. There was an almost vegetable freshness to her, green and gentle. Is this okay? I asked. It feels good, Olivia said. Her body was small. I could feel its smallness even with my finger pads, how she felt dense underneath her skin, intentionally made. She half-turned toward me, eyes still shut. She had tiny nipples, lovely freckles on her torso.

Nathan's presence reminded me how adept he was at claiming Olivia, how nervous I was to try to claim her myself. But her body turned toward me. I recognized it. I remembered what I loved most about being with women: this early space of intimacy that felt lawless and infinite, untethered from any world we knew. She held her eyes shut while she moved herself into my hand. There she was—Olivia—half guarded, half greedy. I felt myself smiling. I moved very slowly. A first-kiss hush grew around us in the room. She grew wider and deeper, grasping. I was warm and sure. The air thickened, the susurrus of Olivia's voice swelled, her breath swelling her rib cage too. Slowly, slowly, as though afraid she would change her mind, I sank into the bed and put my mouth on her clit. She was hot, vegetal, her muscles compact and unpredictable. I held her body against my face. All my insecurities were savaged by the abrupt strength of her body. *There she is, that girl I love.* At some point Nathan rose and guided his cock into her mouth. She accepted him dreamily, almost unconsciously.

Eventually Olivia grew shy and twisted her hips away from me. Olivia—I said.

Oh, no, please, Olivia said as she pulled away from Nathan, I'm embarrassed. She laughed and pulled her hair across her face.

Please—I love getting to touch you—I—

Olivia pulled her shirt down and walked to the kitchen bar to fetch the wine bottle.

Don't you enjoy the way Olivia always adds some dramatic shape to the whole thing? Nathan said softly to me.

I followed Olivia across the small room and she showed me the cabinet above the sink in which she kept four small tumblers for wine. I felt surprisingly powerful. If Nathan touched me in the right place I would ring like a bell. When had I begun to prefer the person I was around them? Despite all my reservations, part of me loved being this girl, not just in my body but in the way we spoke to one another. I had been wrong to imagine that I only wanted to watch their game from the audience.

Nathan, would you like this? Olivia said. How about a cigarette?

I'm fine, Liv, Nathan said, but he sat up and accepted a glass from her. I found my own cigarettes—conscious, as I rummaged through my bag, of the animal bawdiness in my squatted haunches—and offered one to Nathan. He allowed me to light it, draining his glass quickly so as to use it as an ashtray.

How are things with your girlfriend? Nathan said, out of the blue.

I felt a little cold then. It seemed to me again that Romi's name should not even be breathed in a room he inhabited. I couldn't think of her while I was with him, not beyond a flash of tender memory. It was not the case that I had only one life.

Fine, I said, sitting on the bed again.

What's her name again? Nathan said. She has a nice name. Elegant.

I peeled the clementine Olivia had left on the bed and offered Nathan the better part.

Rose? he said. Something like that?

She's fine.

But you just keep coming back to us, don't you, Nathan said.

Yes, I said. I like that you seem to know just what to do with me.

That's Nathan's talent, of course, Olivia said, smiling as she fetched him a second tumbler for wine.

Nathan reached out his hand and I placed the last wedge of clementine into it. This gesture made me intensely aware of our body language, our limbs yellow and gray in Olivia's half-light, my feet tucked beneath me as I faced Nathan. He reclined on the far side of the bed beside the nightstand with its crowd of cups. Olivia sat with her feet hanging off the bed, as though she might need to get up at any moment. A little air came in through the two inches of open window. The mood between us felt achingly tender, the sense of earned leisure exquisite, as though the reward for the long, strange winter was this exact intimacy. I knew this was why I had refilled Nathan's water glass so many times at dinner, why I found the cigarettes for him and peeled the clementine. I had come to this place of communal goodwill, the feeling that we did not antagonize but in fact loved one another.

But what made me think this was love? The caring that Olivia did for Nathan, that I rushed to do for Nathan? Did it remind me of Romi's years of service? Was it any good, this love, if what it meant was that Olivia and I circled Nathan, offering him every service we were capable of?

I thought of a question from the sex-addiction questionnaire that Fatima had pulled up on her phone: *Does your pursuit of sex or sexual fantasy conflict with your moral standards or interfere with your personal spiritual journey? Yes/No.*

Nathan, I said, if you just *know what to do* with me, isn't that just misogyny, in both of us? That I want that, to be fucked by you like that? Me and Olivia?

Nathan was surprised. He handed me the cigarette as though it could pacify me.

Why are you still thinking about all that bullshit? he said. I thought I cured you of that.

My life?

Not your life. Politics. This is your life.

I had meant my question sincerely. I was in the mood to trust in their intentions and allow them into my true thinking. I tried to keep my tone teasing.

This is some hole I crawl into every weekend, I said. And, what, I'm supposed to think that's *empowering*? Getting fucked by you—just because I enjoy it?

In Nathan's silence I leaned over him and dropped the butt in the empty cup. His eyes followed me. As I sat back down I uncrossed my legs so my pussy was wide-mouthed toward him. I didn't look at Olivia, didn't want to know what she felt. I found the lighter where it had fallen onto the bed.

And it's so odd, I said. Olivia and I have relationships with women, we're interested in women! It's not like we thought, *Well, shit—no way around it, we need the dick.* Yet somehow— I should speak for myself. I grew up talking about sex as this thing women should have however they want it, sexual freedom as this great sort of pinnacle beyond morality or anything provincial. So I'm supposed to think I can't damage myself, that things don't hurt me, if I choose them, if I see them clearly? Isn't that just the deepest submission to power? *Here, fine, I can't resist this anymore?*

Don't you enjoy this? Nathan said. Don't you come back here again and again? Don't I make you come like a fucking animal?

Listen—don't think I don't lie awake at night hoping against hope that it'll be a woman I end up with, so that I can look myself in the eye. I know all I've done is entrench myself in an ideological trap just like the one I would have faced fifty years ago, only reversed. But—

But, Eve, Olivia said from behind me.

I turned to look at her. She was red.

Isn't this good? she said. Profoundly good?

She held my eyes. I could see her outside the vulnerable claustrophobia in which we spent all our time together, could see her as she was out in the world, walking into the restaurant that same evening, demure and hopeful, her eyes on the sidewalk.

Doesn't . . . Isn't this a special part of your life? Olivia said. Has it ever been like this for you before?

I knew my answer and yet I couldn't understand it. I had been in love before, was even now in love with Romi, had felt consumed whole by passion. And there were many moments in which I didn't even like Nathan and Olivia, when they seemed to me irredeemably entitled or careless, when I feared that they were privately sadistic. Yet I could not overstate the significance of the experience I had with them. It was as though all the questions I cared most about, and inside which I felt most alone—desire, sex, gender, attention, intimacy, vanity, and power—were placed for display on a table between the three of us. I could study them like fruit in a bowl. I recognized the shapes of these questions, knew my own history with them, and yet when I had encountered them in the past I had been sunk so deep in hope or loyalty, in some delusion, that I had never come close to real comprehension. And now I could sense that clarity was somehow within reach. If I could just stay in the room long enough, walk all the way around the table and see the bowl from every angle, some new possibility for freedom would appear.

I wanted to apologize then, but I knew it would hurt me to do so. Instead I said, Olivia, will you let me know if you want to see me, just the two of us? I'd love that.

Olivia blushed again and nestled beneath Nathan's arm.

It's my birthday next week, I said. I'm having some people over. Maybe you could come.

Olivia lay there like a cat, unmoving.

When we had risen from the bed and dressed and Olivia was in the little kitchen Nathan approached me and held me gently against the wall, his hips just grazing my hips. His hand cradled my head. The sex is so good, I said, because I wanted to apologize, to show him how I felt.

Oh, he said, with feeling, as though he too was baffled.

Do you have some caveat? I asked.

God, no. No, how could I? He ran his hands around my back warmly and roundly, the way someone might if they wanted to comfort you, or the way your boyfriend might if he was loath to be away from your treasured body.

I held him back. With each breath that I took I readied myself for the loss of him, for the awareness that his chest had re-treated an inch. After four breaths I remembered everything.

Are you working all weekend? I said.

Yes. He leaned away from me. I touched my phone. All three of us stood by the door to say goodbye to one another. I tried to kiss Olivia, and Nathan said, Liv, give her a real kiss.

7

Then it was August. Midafternoon. Romi and I had a Saturday to ourselves. We were lying on her bed in our T-shirts and underwear, too flushed to go out anywhere, relishing the cool of the air conditioner. Outside on the street an ice cream truck was singing by.

You want something? Romi said. I'll go get us something.

She disappeared onto the street. Her bed was cool and dry. I was in an unforgivable ecstasy—the ecstasy of having everything I wanted, having more than I had imagined was possible, Nathan and Olivia and Romi. I felt I was approaching something like the feeling I had intuited on meeting Olivia in the bar, all those months ago, when I realized that she was living in a private and spectacular world and that I might be able to enter it.

When Romi brought me a Popsicle I sat up against the wall and bit the top off with a gratified sound. She sat down beside me on the bed.

Do you like doing things for me? I said, while I licked some

Popsicle juice off my hand. I mean, do you get tired of going out to get things, carrying things?

Romi was licking her Popsicle methodically, from bottom to top, rotating it ninety degrees after each assault.

Of course I like it, she said. I don't think about it much.

Do you think that's the difference between a good person and a bad person? That you don't even have to think about what the good thing to do is?

You don't really believe in good people and bad people, Romi said.

On the other hand, sometimes that's the mark of a good person. That you worry about what's good enough. Because it means you care one way or another.

What's this about? Romi said.

What?

Do you have a decision to make? Something you're worried you might get wrong?

No, I said. I just don't know why it doesn't occur to me to, like, make you breakfast every morning.

Romi took the stained Popsicle stick from me and gathered the wrappers to go throw them out, but I tugged her back into bed and pulled the trash from her hand. I leaned over her, spread the clean sides of the wrappers on the floor, and laid the little wooden sticks on top of them. There was sweat on her thighs from when she'd run out to the ice cream truck. I snuck my hand up through the inside of her running shorts. Her underwear was soaked and thick at the crotch, her lips hot.

Oh, don't, Romi said. I'm on my period.

So what?

Romi lowered her eyes. I pushed the tips of my first two fingers against her. I saw her stomach tense, and her eyes pressed close for a moment. Then she put a hand on my wrist and shimmied back, out of my reach.

What?

She crossed her legs. Eve, she said, I want to break up.

Are you serious?

Yes.

I put my head in my hand for a moment, but I saw there was blood on my fingers. I wiped them on the sheets. Who is it? I said.

A colleague, Romi admitted. From the hospital.

In the distance were the sirens that, in my years of confused happiness in the city, I had ceased to notice. Now they came crisply in through the closed windows. The feeling I had was not unlike seeing the bowl in the middle of a room in which Nathan and I were talking. An intense clarity opened up. Everything was thick with light and heat. The beige carpet in Romi's room glowed.

I'm sorry, Romi said. I didn't plan it like this. It got away from me.

It got away from you?

Yes.

Romi looked regretful but resigned, as though surveying a mess on the floor.

It got away from you, I said. So you can get it back. Right?

What do you mean? Romi said. You still want to be together? With what I'm telling you?

Yes.

Are you sure?

The air between us was static. I looked at her, at the carpet, back at her, down at my own hands. Was I sure?

You know I'm not attached to monogamy, I said. People

make mistakes. Or not even mistakes—they want things. That's fine. But that doesn't mean you leave.

You want me to stay?

Of course. What we have—don't you think we should keep it? Isn't that the important thing?

Romi turned her eyes away from me. I really don't think so, she said. I think honesty is the important thing.

I know you think that. That's why I was so sure about you, I said. About everything that had to do with you.

What do you mean?

Well, I was sure you'd never leave me, for one thing.

Romi made a shape with her mouth that I thought might have been the start of a painful laugh, but she quickly straightened her lips. I didn't think I would either, she said.

It's crazy, how sure I was. I mean, I trust you—I trusted you—so much . . .

Because I'm trustworthy, Romi said. Don't you—

Don't touch me, I said.

I started to gather my things. Even while I rushed to leave I had a keen desire to love her, stronger than I had felt since our early days. The degree of clarity in the room was unignorable, like the smell of burning hair. There was nothing that excited me more than revelation.

Is something wrong with me? I asked her. The flurry of movement had unstuck something in my mind. Is that why you decided you could dump me? I said. Did you figure it out?

What are you talking about?

That I fuck men sometimes, I said. That I like men.

It's not your fault, Eve, she said.

What do you mean? Do you know about . . .

Do I know about what? Romi looked at me. I don't know what you're talking about.

No?

I don't know. Why are you asking me? Are you sleeping with someone?

Did you think that, or did I just tell you that?

But then why would you talk to me about *trustworthiness*? If you've been fooling around?

I had my shorts on and my bag in my hands. I squinted through the sun. Her hair was as bright as a lamp.

Come on, Romi, I said. Because you're a trustworthy person. Didn't you just say so? You're a good person. I'm *supposed* to trust you. You told me to. You work with kids! You pick up food for us on the way home from the hospital, for Christ's sake. You never—

I know that you love me, Romi said. Or you think you do. But I think this is sort of how you think of me—like this perfect person. It isn't right. I'm always afraid of disappointing you.

You're afraid of disappointing *me*? That's what this is about?

Romi stood and picked up the trash from beside the bed.

What if I forget to bring an umbrella? she said. What if I'm tired? What if, I don't know, I'm not the perfect girlfriend for a week? What will you think then?

You just said you don't even have to think about those things, you do them without even thinking!

Stop it, Romi said softly. You're bored with me.

Are you kidding?

You don't want to be, but you are. You think, *Well, she's so great, we love each other, how could I possibly be bored.* But you are! Aren't you bored? Isn't that why you did whatever you did?

I didn't think you'd actually leave, I said.

I didn't think you'd fuck someone else.

Yeah, I fucked someone else! So did you!

I didn't fuck— I haven't fucked anyone. Come on. I wouldn't—

Oh, you haven't fucked her? What is it—just breathing on each other, saying how you *wish* you could fuck? Is that it?

Come on. I'm serious. I didn't fuck anyone, I didn't sneak around, I didn't lie. I haven't betrayed you. But I'm telling you— I feel—I know it's worse this way, in a way, it's easier to stomach if it's something terrible, but I didn't—

I fucked someone, Romi, but I'd never leave. Never.

Romi crushed the Popsicle wrappers and sticks in her fist and walked into the bathroom. Why do you think that's any better? she said through the doorway. You'd rather lie? Is that what you want to go around doing—lying and pretending? I heard her turn the shower on. She stood on the threshold. Is that what you want to do? Does that make you feel good, Eve?

—

At least you don't call yourself trustworthy, Fatima said. Isn't that strange? How Romi really believes she's so upstanding? Even though she's been fucking around with some woman?

In love with some woman, I corrected her. I don't even know that they've slept together yet. Maybe she hasn't done anything wrong.

But she left you, Fatima said.

I don't think it's strange that Romi believes the best about herself, I said. It makes perfect sense. It's why *I* believed in her, why she made me feel so grounded and sure about things. Because she doesn't allow herself any doubt. She was so confused about why I wouldn't trust her, even when she told me she was leaving me! For someone else! She couldn't imagine that she could be a bad person in this scenario. Or ever.

You're overthinking it, Fatima said. Fact is: She isn't who you thought she was. That's it.

Maybe not. But I'm not who she thought I was either.

All right, Eve. That's what a breakup is. You learn some things, you change your life.

But I *didn't* change my life.

No. It's been changed for you. And for the better, in my book.

You don't like Romi?

That's not what I said, Fatima said. I don't have a problem with Romi. But I don't like all this bullshit about Romi being such a great gift to the world—and you being lucky to lick her boots.

She's a fucking doctor! She was a truly shining example— come on, you've hardly ever had a boyfriend as selfless as Romi.

I couldn't care less. It's just no good, thinking that way about your girlfriend. It ruins your life. I don't like to see you like that. Acting like a woman living beyond your means, always grateful to Romi, always shocked she still loves you.

—

There were tears and hiccups, panic attacks in the back seats of cabs, sleepless nights. It was very hot all month, and the city smelled like meat and sewage. Fatima made iced tea in large pitchers. Some afternoons she woke me with ice on my neck and inside my ears.

Occasionally she succeeded in convincing me to come outside and smoke on the stoop.

I don't think you have much *besides* doubt, Fatima said as she placed the ashtray between us. I laughed and my laughter pushed the tears waiting in my eyes onto my face. She said, Isn't it exhausting—being wiser than everyone else?

A few days later a small purple box arrived. Fatima brought it in to me. Inside was a long, tangled piece of jewelry that

Fatima and I were baffled by in our heat-soaked, muddled state. Finally Fatima said, after she had coiled it around her neck three times, Oh! Do you think it's a body chain?

A long row of little gold plates wound down a central chain that floated, once we had untangled it, between my breasts, then split into twin threads strung over each hip. We looked at it, suspended across my dirty T-shirt. It made us both laugh for the first time in days.

There's a note, Fatima said. Did you see it? *Belated happy birthday. My pleasure, N.*

She laughed again. He's really something, isn't he.

I knew from her tone that I should be ashamed, but all I felt was a sort of surprised gratitude that I still existed to someone other than Fatima. I put the chain in my underwear drawer and forgot about it. Nathan was a mirage of hope and vanity— luxuries I could no longer afford.

———

In the evenings I felt Romi's absence as a soreness in the muscles of my chest and arms. Or perhaps it wasn't Romi's absence I felt but the absence of that belief that I might someday be as loving and devoted as Romi had been. Is it possible to nurture a love that is not a referendum on yourself? At what stage in life is a person capable of such a feeling? In Romi's absence all the shelters had been taken down, not just the shelters in which I was living but every building in the country where I lived, every possible warm room, and they would not be rebuilt in my lifetime. She had left because I was selfish—because I was incapable of generous love. Further proof: I wanted something bad, but not too bad, to befall her. I wanted her commute to be slowed to an hour each day while the train stopped in a tunnel beneath the river. And if it was the case that she was not so good as I had imagined, that she was as fallible as the rest of us, what comfort could I take in that? It only meant the end of a dream I had had, a dream of selfless love.

Fatima left glasses of iced tea on my nightstand that sweated and formed rings on the wood. Once or twice a day I would sit in the shower under lukewarm water for half an hour. Why had I ever thought of the love I had grown for Romi as such a deep good? Now that my love had no object I was aware of it in a new way. It was much larger than I had thought—huge—slow and sensitive, like a great jellied creature floating around in me, bumping up against fear or doubt or narcissism and bouncing off, gently bruised, toward a corner that might be more accommodating. I had to find a place for it, but it was too big, too alien. And what good was my love, anyway? A love in which I had lied and hoped, by way of lying, to be redeemed? What good I could create in myself was unrecognizable.

8

Isn't this nice, Olivia said. Meeting like this normally? As though we're just normal people in the world?

She held her arms close to her body when she spoke, as if nervous she might get in someone's way, though the bar was fairly empty. It was a Monday evening on the Upper East Side. She'd told me she had an errand to run in this neighborhood after work.

I'm so glad, I said. It is nice. Seeing you in the real world, alone.

Nathan suggested we finally do it. I got a raise and he said, Why don't you buy Eve a drink?

It had been two weeks since Romi had left me. I was a dishtowel that had been soaked and wrung out again and again. The reminder of Nathan and Olivia's presence in my life—that I had not lost them in the same breath that I lost Romi—felt like a real surprise to me. More than I deserved.

Olivia and I ordered gin cocktails.

I think we have similar taste, I ventured.

She braided her hair quietly.

So, I said. How are you?

I've been, I don't know, I've been a little anxious.

At work?

No. With my paintings. I'm planning for a show. It's not till next year, but, you know—I showed some paintings to Nathan, I wanted his opinion. And he liked them, I guess. But—Olivia made a small, demure gesture, and her drink sloshed a little in her hand—it feels awful, showing things to him.

Why? He's unkind?

No, of course not. It's just that it's so important that he understand it.

And he didn't?

He's honest, she said after a moment. I think he likes the paintings, likes them fine. But he's outside it. Distant. And I'm so used to thinking he's a part of it, because he's in my mind, you know, or because I'm painting him.

I never got the impression he was as interested in art as you are, I said. So maybe he's just—you know—not as expert.

Olivia took a long sip of her drink. He's been really useful to me, she said. Sometimes, you know, on the right day, he can help me out of a kind of . . . I don't know . . . a bluntness, a boredom that I feel with it. Not knowing where to go.

But not this time?

She stayed quiet, toying with her napkin.

What is it? I said. Tell me.

There isn't anything, Olivia said.

Well—he's involved in everything you do, I said gently. I imagine that must be hard. Especially when you feel some kind of distance.

A familiar look, as though she was swallowing her words,

thinking better of them. And then shame floating quickly across her features. He's just been busy, she said. You know how sometimes he disappears. And I've been having a bit of a hard time lately.

She blinked quickly, as though to disappear spots from her vision, and shook her head with a small smile.

Listen, she said, how are you? Tell me something about your life, anything. I feel like you're always interrogating us.

I hope I interrogate Nathan more than you.

He enjoys it, Olivia said kindly.

I'm fine. The summer hasn't been easy for me either. But I'm all right.

What happened?

I thought about it for a moment. Was there any harm in telling Olivia something true about my life? At one point I might have thought she was liable to dredge it up as a weapon in a moment of anger. But here she was, talking to me about her work as she had been so unwilling to do before. Perhaps, instead, it would help her to trust me.

My girlfriend and I broke up, I said. A few weeks ago.

Olivia placed her hands palm-down and kneaded the tabletop with her fingertips. I'm so sorry, Eve, she said. I'm really sorry.

Thank you.

She sipped her drink and stared into the glass instead of at me. When she looked up it was with that deliberate set to her mouth that had struck me in our first meeting, back in December.

How do you feel? she said.

I knew I wouldn't be able to answer her without crying, so I sat very still.

I guess that's the wrong question, she said. I'm sorry, I know it's awful.

Thinking about it, I probably shouldn't have been so shocked, I said. But I was. I was really shocked.

Oh, Eve.

Isn't that odd? I shook my head a little to discourage my teariness and said, after a moment, Have you ever had a breakup you were really shocked by?

No. Not yet.

Olivia, I said, if it ever were to end between the two of you—if you don't mind my asking—how do you think it would end? Have you ever thought about it?

Yes, she said. She looked downward, into her drink. I don't know how. When I think about it, that's when I start to get, you know . . . a little nervous.

I wanted to tell her all the reasons I thought she had to be afraid. How sometimes, even in my other world, brushed only occasionally by Nathan's fingers, I too was afraid. But I tried to listen—I wanted her to trust me. I reached my hand toward her and let it lie on the table.

I do think, you know, if it ended, I would have to leave my job, she said. That's how it would end. And I don't want to, not at all. When we first met you, and things had just started between us, I thought it was a small thing. I have my work—I could do any job. Right? And I wanted to fuck Nathan so badly, I would have done anything for it—seriously, I was crazy about it, I didn't care what happened. In fact (now Olivia grinned at me shyly), I made a whole list of all the reasons he could find for why we shouldn't and how I could refute them all.

Did you show it to him?

Not until later on.

And now you're not so sure you'd want to leave your job?

I don't know, Olivia said. I can't really think about it ending. When I do, I sort of . . . lose my sense of things. I get so anxious. You know—freak out. Nathan has to be very firm with me, tell me that I'm being crazy, tell me not to worry. And in these very particular moments—you know—when I'm really freaked out—

She paused, picked up her drink, and set it down again. She seemed surprised to be admitting this.

When I'm really freaked out sometimes, I get very angry at him. I almost hate him. You know. Or I do hate him. Because everything is his—my whole life. . . . I think I told you I dated this boy in college. He was horrible to me. Just cruel, abusive, he treated me horribly. I can't really explain it all. But, you know, I do think sometimes I'm attracted to this—to giving myself up to something like this . . . something consuming. With its own rules.

Someone like Nathan.

No one is like Nathan.

No, I said, smiling so she might continue.

Nathan isn't like that, Olivia said. He cares so much. But you're right that I'm devoted to him in a different way—and that he can do anything he wants, that everything I do depends on him. And at work too, I care so much about the work and I love working with him and then, of course, if he wanted me gone I would just have to go.

I felt a warm, lucid care for her. All the concern I remembered from the early weeks we'd spent together, when I had first tried to parse the relationship between her and Nathan, was collecting heavily in my mouth. I looked at her and waited. If there was any way I could be a friend to her, I thought, I would give

Nathan up as quickly as I'd found him; I would do my best to bring her into a gentler world.

But what was I waiting for her to confess, what help did I think she would ask for? Hadn't I seen her maneuver her way into Nathan's life with my own eyes? She wanted nothing to do with a gentler world. That was my fantasy, a fantasy in which I was innocent because Olivia was safe.

Finally I said, Don't you ever think, I don't know . . . do you ever think that you'll just be together? Openly?

No. No, never.

Why not?

Oh, I don't know. I can't say. I've known him for so long. Olivia looked down at my hand and shook her head. You know, Nathan is incredibly generous, incredibly patient, she continued. And he's shown me what kind of person I want to be. Before . . . You didn't know me, but before I started up with Nathan I wasn't alive in the same way. I thought I was, but it was a joke. I get so nervous to show the paintings to him now, because these are really who I am—who I am when I'm alone. And they're about him, of course. About this overwhelming thing that has overtaken my life. Being with him. And that's why, you know, I didn't want to talk to you about the paintings you saw. Because sometimes you say these things—about how I am with him—and it makes me wonder, it makes me see things with Nathan in a totally different way. I care what you think. But I don't . . .

What?

The way you see things—

Nathan, I said.

I was surprised to see Nathan appear behind Olivia, wearing a small smile. He took off his jacket.

Hello, I said. What are you doing here?

It's lovely to see you, Eve, he said. Olivia? Would you like another drink?

Yes, thank you, she said.

Nathan pulled up a third chair, on which he hung his jacket, and went to the bar.

I'm so annoyed with him, Olivia said. I didn't know he was going to show up so soon.

She gave me a mischievous smile. I felt like an eighth-grader with a new best friend, planning to shoplift lip glosses after school.

Oh, so you like being alone with me?

Yes, Olivia said. Now I'm annoyed that I won't get to talk to you.

You can talk to me, I said. I love talking to you. You were telling me about the way I see things. It upsets you.

No, Olivia said. It doesn't. It just—it just interests me. But we don't need to—

Would you like to share this one with me, Eve? Nathan said. He sat down with two drinks and set one in front of Olivia and the other between us.

What are you doing here so early? Olivia said.

Look, she isn't even happy to see me, Nathan said to me.

But I'm happy to see you, I said. I was. My heart and my sex were running confused circles around each other at the sight of his hands, his distracted face as he finished a message on his phone and returned it to his pocket. I knew I was forsaking Olivia—forsaking her even in turning toward him with a smile—and I couldn't stop myself. I pushed my hair behind my ear and waited to be struck down.

—

I could watch Nathan and Olivia having sex but watching them kiss made me near sick. Nathan was a skilled kisser, capable of soft control. When they kissed she was a supplicant and he was boundlessly merciful. He was always above her, holding her head, bearing her softly against him.

I heard Olivia's voice break the kiss: Will you turn the lights down?

I went to the threshold of the room and found the switch. She was lying in the cradle of his body on the couch, face against his chest, only his hand grasping the back of her neck. It was stunning how she loved him, how lying against him seemed to undo her. Small moans like whispers escaped her while his hand kneaded her neck. The Emeralite lamps bled yellow light but their small rectangular nests were lurid green. I was reminded of how I felt in libraries: quick, awestruck, aware that this scale of knowledge was a freedom so great I would have disbelieved it had I not been born into its public shelter. On a side table beside our half-empty glasses were two fat copies of John Berger's *Portraits*.

Come sit with us, Nathan said.

I never felt stranger than in the moments in which I attempted to give Olivia privacy in her transparent love and Nathan saw that I needed reassurance. I didn't want to need it and yet my gratitude toward him threatened my clarity. While he was turned toward Olivia I had a small, precious distance. I could see his body harboring his power. When the beam of his attention fell on me I could only perceive the force of his control, an emphatic moon that found me no matter where I stood.

That evening Nathan wore glasses I had not seen before, narrow and frameless, the sort that failed to disappear. They made him look spent. He adjusted Olivia so as to hold my waist. I sat cross-legged, facing him. Sometimes I could forget that he was a desiring man, an imperfectly made agent of his own life and wishes. He convinced me in the way he spoke and held me that every moment was engineered expressly for my variety of pleasures, mine and Olivia's. He looked at me, with my crossed legs, my elbow resting on the back of the couch, as I attempted to convey ease as well as interest. I saw a flicker of a smile: My efforts amused him.

By now I felt so disarmed that when he looked at me I was not only satisfied but confused. Was his lust not genuine, was it only what he knew I hoped for? He was not truly selfless; there was something in it he enjoyed. But was it the sex itself or the ease with which he manipulated me?

We had sex in the engrossing way we sometimes did: unspeaking, at Nathan's direction. He knew by the shape of my body the moment at which I felt utterly defenseless toward him. I trembled. When he sensed that I would come violently Nathan pulled away from me and at the other end of the couch positioned Olivia in front of him.

I groaned, shook my legs. I hated her then. It made me angry, the precision of his control, how he enjoyed the certainty of his power even more than he enjoyed bestowing pleasure. Under Nathan's touch Olivia was pliant, calm. No—I didn't want to feel him turn away from me, as from something shiny toward something deep. I had enjoyed being no more than a beauty to him but now it hurt me to remember that this was all I was. Was it because I wasn't capable of that submission Olivia performed so easily, because I couldn't let him hit me, because I still protected myself by instinct?

I watched Olivia closely. No matter how I arranged my body

to give it to Nathan, in the moment he bent over me, my energy roiled, it was restless and terrible, it displaced my breath and organs. I felt shaken by desire as it passed through me. Olivia's desire was so smooth, so pure. When he hit her she arched and absorbed it as a sea absorbs rain. I could see that it was a momentary call to immense depths concealed in her body. Purpose overcame her at Nathan's touch; her body calmed; she looked full. Safe. Was this love?

It was when I touched her that I felt Olivia's desire and her anxiety roped together. While she finished Nathan with her mouth I knelt behind her, running my fingers over her narrow back, her freckled hips. She moved her knees apart to make space for me and I could feel the urgency and unease in her legs, in the way she adjusted her position once, twice. She grew eager for my hand but her eagerness was almost resentful. While I fingered her I felt as though she was performing willingness, moving only as much as politeness required. And then her desire began in earnest—surprised, even grudging. I could not pull her inside it powerfully, as Nathan did for me. Even so I enjoyed her surprise. *So often when you come it's a complete surprise to you,* I remembered Nathan saying to me, with approval, as though my artlessness made me a proper woman.

The mood was heavy when Nathan came. Olivia was bleeding tenderness and I felt reduced, strange, a body that had given what it could. My own tenderness was of no use to them. Useless to them, useless to Romi. I disguised it as far as I was able.

I chose the role of the spoiled girl; it allowed me some dignity.

You left me hanging, I said.

I did.

I like when he does that to you.

Nathan passed a hand over his face. He removed his glasses and rubbed his eyes.

Work has been very intense this week, he said. Forgive me.

I refilled our glasses from the bottle on the table. It had warmed.

Everything all right?

Oh, yes, Nathan said. Just planning a trip. For work, to London. Establishing an office to handle the UK assets. But Olivia's bitter, he said, smiling wearily at her, because she's not going.

Why not?

Her job isn't relevant.

I could make myself useful, Olivia said.

We can't pay five grand, Nathan said to me, for her to come out, when she simply isn't needed. It'd just be a little vacation for her.

And for you, she said.

I hesitated for a moment. What was the limit of what I could say to them? To what extent did they enjoy my occasional disdain, the way I liked to pretend they disgusted me, as I wished they did?

Isn't it true, I said, that you don't really *need* to do anything you do? I mean, what will anyone notice if you spend five grand on a work trip? Isn't your whole job trying to figure out what to do with excess money? It can't be more immoral to bring Olivia on a work trip than to do half of the other shit you do.

What is it you think we do, Eve? Nathan said. I'm interested.

I don't know. Throw money at lawyers. Investment bankers. Gallerists, auctioneers. Create trusts. Come up with clever tax-fraud schemes. Aren't I close?

And what is it you do again? Olivia said.

Fuck you.

I'm not being an asshole, Olivia said, her tone uncannily like Nathan's. I'm not ragging on your job. People can do what they want, whatever works for them—I'm not interested in faultfinding or whatever. But, you know, I don't have too much patience for this. For being criticized for wading into things, trying to solve problems, by someone who doesn't want to engage with anything complex or dirty. I know a lot of people like you. I've dated them. You just want to keep your hands clean.

There's nothing noble about how I make money, I said. And, sure, we're all implicated one way or another. But you're collapsing very real distinctions. There *are* jobs that don't involve throwing around money and playing God.

What should we be doing? Nathan said.

All I'm saying is, the jobs exist. You have the educations for them.

What should we be doing? Nathan said again.

Well, my girlfriend—she was—she's a pediatrician, I said. That's pretty fucking noble.

Talk about playing God, Olivia said softly, her eyes trained on the wall. Nathan laughed.

Eve, come on, you're smarter than that, he said. There are worthwhile ways to spend your life—career and noncareer related—and plenty of "noble" jobs. But you know the main ones people like to tout—doctors, judges, humanitarians—it's a fallacy that those jobs are noble. The prestige is far more significant than any moral good you might do. Right? For any prestigious job like that, well paid at a good hospital, whatever it is, there are hundreds of people wishing and hoping to do the same work, probably capable of doing it just as well as you could. And if you *are* doing that job, on the top of the do-gooder food chain, it's almost certainly because you had some advantages. Nathan smiled. You should be exhorting us to be teachers or social workers, he said. Doing work people actually need done.

True, I said. Why don't you become a teacher, or a social worker?

I used to teach, Nathan said, with a noncommittal shrug.

What did you teach?

He used to teach art, after he graduated, Olivia said. Before he decided he had bigger plans.

Liv, you aren't coming on this trip, it's that simple, Nathan said.

I think you should tell Nathan he's not being fair, Eve. That you think he should bring me along.

I felt Olivia's undivided charm in the wake of her annoyance, her smile a dare, her cheeks pink. I recognized this look as one often directed toward Nathan. She had none of Nathan's nonchalance—the charm was in the quickening in her voice, her sudden single-mindedness. What affection I felt toward them both then, despite the nature of the argument: how Olivia offered me an olive branch and Nathan, sweetly, imagined that perhaps I was afraid to choose a side. I burned with shame re-membering the scene at the bar just hours earlier, when my pussy had opened at the sight of his hands.

Really? Nathan said to Olivia. You're going to bully Eve until she's on your side?

She's already on my side. I should get to go. Eve agrees. Don't you?

Right about now, I said, is when you might as well sue Na-than. Don't you think you could make a case out of this? He's your boss, he's fucking you, and now—

I would never sue Nathan. Olivia blushed. That's absurd.

If you did, I said, you could call me as a witness, no hesitation. I mean it.

I laughed to show them I meant them no harm, but I kept my eyes on Olivia. The sting of danger moved across the back of my neck. I had shown her that I understood the stakes, that when they shook out I would not hesitate.

Olivia would never sue me, Nathan said. If I thought she would, I'd sue her first. Yes, Liv—because you seduced me! It's true. You'd have to say so under oath.

I'm pretty sure that doesn't matter at all, I said, given that she works for you.

I would never sue Nathan, Olivia said again. Why would you even mention that?

Nathan, she *works for you.*

Jesus Christ, Nathan said. You don't understand.

Sure, sure, I said, I'm sure I don't.

Honestly, Olivia said, I think this is juvenile. She put down her glass. I do, she continued, I do think it's juvenile. It's not obvious the way you think it is. . . . The rules don't apply. Yes, we work together. Yes, I see why that can be sticky—why people worry about that kind of thing. But the work feeds off the sex feeds off the work. That's what makes it good work—or at the very least that's what makes it interesting. I don't have to justify this to you. But intimacy has its own fruit, particular fruit. It's idiotic to think these boundaries between work and life are obvious. Or that they're useful. No one looks at the Bloomsbury group and says, *What a mistake, they shouldn't have all been fucking, Keynes and Woolf and Leonard,* do they? Listen— I know I'm not Virginia Woolf. I'm not saying that. But my work has been so much deeper—being with Nathan inspires me, he's given me so much I want to express. I do finally have a show going up. Next year. I don't need to tell you this. But what you're thinking of is parochial. It's not real.

I could feel Olivia trying to erase what little she might have implied to me in the bar.

Maybe that's half true, I said to her. But listen. Nathan *does* have all the power here. You have to admit it. You enjoy that about being underneath him, working underneath him.

Of course, Nathan said. But we agreed to this. This thing of yours, your qualms—it's so boring. It has nothing to do with us.

Look, I said to Olivia, we're both queer. Yet here we are. I'm trying to understand why I want this.

Olivia frowned at me. With Nathan?

Obviously you have this . . . incomparable confidence, I said to Nathan. An insane confidence. But the way you use it—it's coercive.

Nathan laughed.

I'm not saying I haven't wanted everything. I have. I love it. You know I love it. But you do coerce us. Right up to the edge.

I don't, Nathan said. I just know what you want.

Remember the first time you talked me into not using a condom? You were about to fuck me, and I said, *Do you have a condom?* You just kept asking, *Do you really want me to get it, do you really want me to,* until I just—

You didn't want me to use one, Nathan said.

I asked you—

Tell me honestly, Nathan said. Isn't it true that you didn't want me to use one?

I asked you to get one.

Eve, Nathan said. Isn't that what you wanted?

Yes, I said slowly.

Isn't it true you didn't want me to use a condom?

Yes.

Didn't you like it that way—that I pushed you?

Yes.

You wanted it just like that.

Yes, I said. I thought I would cry. The truth of it felt miserable, impossible, ecstatic.

I know, Nathan said. I knew. It's not coercion, not at all. Not a little bit. I know what you want, and I give it to you. You're different than Olivia, what you want is different, it's sort of surface. You're afraid of it, but I can sense it. That's what I did.

I hated that he named me this way and yet my spirit rose to his words. I recognized them in a way I had only recognized love or music, those seeds whose twins in you are so strong that it feels heretical to deny them. I hated him and I was grateful to him for telling me what I was unwilling to name, I needed it named, I wanted to put it in the bowl on a table so that it could finally be consecrated or destroyed.

I have a sense of certain things, Nathan said. When you fuck it can happen one of two ways. Sometimes you force it out of yourself, you make it happen. Other times—this is the thing that interests me—it's completely involuntary, you have no conscious part in it, it happens no matter what you do. It's absolute. The cuckold doesn't truly want to be cuckolded, it's humiliating, it ruins his life. But despite that witnessing it makes him come involuntarily. He can't help it in the least. He comes even against his will. When I first fucked you—you know this—that was what it was.

I thought of the conversations I had with Fatima when she asked me what it was like with Nathan and Olivia. *It's baffling,* I remembered saying to her. *I say things I can't believe, things I*

*know are stupid or that I'm ashamed of. I even start to hate Olivia!
And then I want more.*

We can't talk about that kind of thing directly, Nathan said.
Can't pull back the curtain. You can ruin it.

Nathan is always like this, Olivia said. Her voice surprised
me. I was aware of her then only as a kind of surveillance. He's
sort of proprietary, she said. But we can forgive him, because
he's so good at it.

Most people are impossible, Nathan said. When you talk to
them it's absolutely tedious. You don't get at who they are at all.
At best they're recycling lines from *The Atlantic,* at worst from
the *Post.* They aren't honest—they don't know what they're
doing, they've just picked up all these little signals as to how to
act. But when you *fuck* them—everyone is interesting to fuck.
Everyone. Olivia, do you have my cigarettes?

Olivia found her bag and rummaged in it.

I don't mean kink or anything like that, Nathan went on.
Thank you, Liv. No, nothing so straightforward. What I mean
is, when someone fucks, they are working, most people, with
a scant category of experience and language. When you first
fuck them people do what they think they should do, but they
don't really *know* what they should do. They have far less experience at it than they do at talking. And the variety of things
that are acceptable, or *exciting,* is so much more vast. So they
have a small lexicon of ways they think they should behave but
they aren't certain, and usually they aren't nearly as practiced
at it as they are at bullshitting. It's all interesting, because the
things they *think* they should do are fascinating—they're surprisingly specific, it's not a universal language—and then, once
you figure out what they really want, that's just lovely. Both
elements, and the contrast between them too, whatever that
gap is.

I looked over at Olivia. She glowed. In the pause in conversation she reached over to light Nathan's cigarette and then cradled the lighter in her lap, absently peeling its price sticker. Nathan's interested in everyone, she said. Even the most boring, the most self-involved people. It's really generosity, that's what it is, this endless generosity and interest. Well—Nathan smiled at her—just not in a dinner conversation, she added.

Like this girl I saw last month, Nathan said, ashing into a cup on the side table. Jenny. Right, Liv? She's absolutely boring. She likes to be abject—always getting on her knees. But you can't take her to dinner.

Can she tell you don't respect her? I said.

Yes.

Does she like it, do you think?

Yes! Nathan said. God yes, she likes it—that's what's fun about it. How many times do I have to tell you I'm not a sadist?

Listen, I said. You know I'm interested in that gap between what you think you should do or think you should want, whatever it is, and what you really want. I love that you can figure it out. I want you to tell me what it is, for me. Just—tell me.

You can ruin it. Like I said.

You won't ruin anything. It isn't a fucking magic trick. I need to know.

That's exactly what it is. A magic trick. You can't pin it. It dies.

I was afraid but the fear was like the fear of marriage or rapture—a rich fear that begs to be overcome.

Tell me, I said. I need to figure it out and handle it.

It can't be handled.

He found his glasses on the table and put them on.

And it isn't this simple, he said. You know that. There's no one I could look at, that anyone could look at, to distill their sexuality into a couple of paragraphs. Succinctly, clearly. I'm better at it than most, but it can't be done—that's why people are interesting sexually even when they're uninteresting in other ways. We're not socialized into it as thoroughly as we are into everything else, into daily life. We have ideas but we haven't had the chance to bear them all out or understand them properly. It's not as though I could map it out for you.

Nathan, I said, couldn't you just tell me what it is, whatever theory you have about my sexuality? I know you have one. It wouldn't ruin anything. I have my own ideas, but I need to know what you think.

It's no good to do this, he said. You can't reduce things, can't pick them apart. Why do you want to kill it?

Just fucking talk to me!

You're different from Olivia, Nathan said. Even though you like some of the same things. Olivia isn't afraid of what she wants. She follows it all the way down. Goes as deep as she can.

Olivia sat at the far end of the couch, playing with the tips of her hair. Her eyes fixed on Nathan. She held her knees to her chest.

What am I afraid of?

You just looked at Olivia, Nathan said. You're looking at her all the time. Do you know? Because you're afraid of her judgment, her feelings, whatever. But she's seen all this. She's seen me fuck you. She knows.

I know, I said.

First of all, you have a straightforward rape fantasy.

Fuck you.

You're too afraid to get near it, Nathan said. Rape. Submission. Too anxious about it. Surface.

Whereas Olivia is just totally comfortable with the fact that she wants to be humiliated?

Comfortable doesn't come into it, Eve, Nathan said. Look at Olivia. Does Olivia look comfortable to you? Olivia isn't comfortable with anything. Olivia isn't comfortable for a minute. Comfortable doesn't have anything to *do* with sex—do you understand?

But she doesn't hate what she wants! I said. She doesn't hate you!

You don't hate me.

I should. Haven't you been fucking with me this whole time? Haven't you been—

Challenging you is not the same as violating you.

I hope you don't think you've ruined anything, I said finally. By telling me this.

Not at all, Nathan said lightly, as though I had asked him if he wouldn't mind holding a door for me. If I wasn't so tired, I'd fuck you again.

I pulled on my clothes, sure this was my cue to leave. I was aware of how easily I might lose sight of myself and melt into his authority. I had forgotten Olivia was there and I regretted naming her desire, even while it was obvious. Something had come loose in me. Clearly in Romi's absence I was volatile. When I stood Nathan laughed.

Why are you laughing?

I'm laughing at how you always leave, Nathan said. It's very sweet. It's obvious that you want to stay.

I just don't want to overstay my welcome.

It's always so vulnerable, Nathan said. You're most vulnerable when you go to leave.

I was gutted by this of all things. Not one hour of my life

spent making myself into a woman who held her own, who entered and left rooms as she pleased, had any weight.

Should I stay?

I'll let you know when it's time for you to leave. Come sit down.

I felt an almost painful relief. My body knew only how to hold on to itself, how to stay awake and breathe. I was the self I had become under his words—*rape fantasy, always so vulnerable*—stripped of my illusions and defenses. I was wet immediately. Nathan placed his hand on my thigh and each time I found him looking at me my breath flushed completely out of my belly, rapid and uncontrolled. I could only hold my hand over my mouth, hold my eyes shut. Nathan's hand moved under my shirt and I felt it palpating quickly as my ribs rose and sank. I heard a wet sound—Olivia's mouth. I couldn't open my eyes to him, my eyelids were my only guard.

Do you want me to fuck you, Nathan said.

I wanted to cry, I felt that I would cry or kick him if he toyed with me further. If he didn't fuck me I would disintegrate. I could only whimper. I was humiliated, desperate, I didn't know how to move, I was only in the darkness of Nathan's hand.

Yes, Nathan said. I felt him above me, his hands moving over my waist, his knees between my knees. Yes, yes, he said. He spoke to me very softly, a murmur, a lyric, like he was drawing it out of my cheek. Yes, yes. It was me that was saying yes, he was saying it for me because I could not trust my mouth. When Nathan entered me my hips moved up to swallow him, breath expelled. I was ragged. There was a pale, holiday ringing of glass—the lips of our glasses on the side table kissing as the couch moved. The whole world was in that sound. I remembered it suddenly. Park Avenue, glasses and bowls, cabs rounding 83rd below us in the late hush, obeying the hour. Our enduring rivers moving vastly around me even while I forgot them.

Don't you want me to come inside you? Nathan's voice. Would you like that?

I exhaled. I was a wire floating in the dark.

She likes that. She told me.

I breathed into my belly.

Would you like that, Eve?

Yes.

Do you want him to come inside you? Olivia's voice.

It's yours.

Don't bullshit, Nathan said.

Admit it, Olivia said.

Admit it!

Yes.

You want it? Say so.

I want it.

No, you can't, I'll be too jealous.

Liv, I want it this way.

Come on, Nathan! Please—

Liv, I want it this way.

Okay, Olivia said, in the voice she used in our cocktail conversations. A voice unsure of its reality.

My body was beyond my control but the words seemed to matter.

Are you sure, I said.

Yes.

Are you sure, Olivia?

She's sure, Nathan said.

—

When Nathan came I began to wrestle with him. I pummeled his chest with my knuckles and shoved my knees one after another into his stomach. You're an asshole, I said to him.

Nathan smiled and raised his hips. I hit him again and again. His arms restrained me, his head bent over my chest. His cock was only a half-limp shadow sheltered between his legs but he stayed strong above me, rocking his body up and down, moving quiet and unceasing against my clit while I flailed. Fuck you! I said. The worm of his cock was warm and I felt, impossibly, like I had to take it inside me again. He rocked and rocked. Fuck you. He moved his head up to rest it against mine, our ears touching. My hair grew wet with his sweat. I kicked my calves against him, tried to get my knees under his chest again, but my arms were pulling his hips toward me like a cure. He held himself just away from me. He was so ripe with sweat I could hardly find any leverage. He smelled like bitter licorice, earthy, like effort, smelled nothing like Romi. Romi's cock was there behind my eyes, the hang of it below her navel during the afternoon, the ribbons of sun on the smooth silicone head, her thighs with their tiny blond hairs. Nathan rocked, rocked, he was impervious to my hatred or my want. I was in the wilds and I could not shock him. No cultivated acquiescence, no charming desire, only rage, only grief—he held his lips against my neck and I felt the hot tip of his tongue. Fuck you! I said. I thrust myself up against him and the head of his cock entered me mildly, like a swollen thumb, then disappeared.

I squirmed out from under him and sat at the edge of the couch. My body coursed and glowed with anger. It was surreal to act exactly as I felt, my soul ecstatic, as clean and true as when I first blurted to Romi that I loved her. I was a perfect vessel, empty. Behind me I heard the two of them murmuring to each other. I walked out of the room and into the darkened foyer.

Weak light framed the room's threshold. From inside I heard, faintly, Olivia's soft croak of love. It was an easy way out—imagining that it was Nathan I hated, imagining that I was a person who was degraded instead of sanctified by Nathan's sex. I was not so different from Olivia. I would never be finished with Nathan of my own volition.

9

In Park Slope there was a vacant lot, big and overgrown, sandwiched between two brownstones. I liked to stand in front of it. The grass there grew waist-high. Floating squares of concrete and tools with painted red handles emerged out of the wild shrubs like some kind of farm imitation. From Grand Army Plaza I could see across to the cars parked on Eighth Avenue and above them the sky to the west. In the end of the Brooklyn summer the air was a friendly blue, growing greener as it deepened, as though the breeze were rushing through the gates of the park and turning everything lush and fragrant. I sat on the half wall in front of this lot, smoking or not smoking, as the light seeped out of the sky and into the ground. I wasn't going to text him.

—

I wasn't going to text him. I had decided. But every time I checked my phone I expected that he would have texted me—

never mind that in the weeks since I had last walked out of his apartment his name hadn't appeared once. And if he did text me I would have the pleasure of ignoring it. There was no reason for me to see him. I was only a toy to him, a toy that would end up crushed under his foot.

Then whenever I allowed myself a cigarette in front of the vacant lot I would think, as I clicked the lighter: *Anytime I want, I can forsake this dinner party and jump into real life.* All right, so I wasn't supposed to want to see him, but that wasn't real life, was it. Real life wasn't Nathan's life, but then again it wasn't this return to self-denial either. Had anyone intuited my needs or met them as Nathan had? With him I was able to admit the extent of my doubts, the side of me that hated him and relished my own hatred as evidence of something discerning and noble. It was comforting to say that I loved what Nathan provided me, and not the man himself. But wasn't that the nature of all love? Gratitude, for how we had been made to feel?

———

I asked myself whether I would see him and flipped a coin: Heads was no, tails yes. When the quarter landed on heads I was desolate for a split second before I realized I was free: I would see him, I would see him no matter what. The bowl appeared again at the edge of my vision. The bowl lived in Nathan's apartment, in rooms Nathan frequented. I could forget about it while I was buying produce and sending letters. Its presence was like an itch or a task I had avoided for so many months it had grown mammoth and accusatory. In my dreams it was always behind me: I could see only the color and grain of the bowl, and in the sheets my body tossed and craned.

I made it another month before I texted him. It was the first time I had requested to see him. Nathan liked it. He liked change, I thought; he liked watching something move, grow, remake itself under his thumb. *You're greedy, aren't you?*

———

In October he came to my apartment. While I stood in the doorway and listened to his shoes on the stairs I felt the sharp awareness that this was my real life, that it would be my real life as soon as he walked through the door. Nathan would no longer be confined to places I remembered for no reason other than that he had provided them. When I remembered what had occurred in the place that I lived in all the years that I lived in it, the memory of him would announce itself on the couch and the bed, on the square of tile in front of the sink.

His face on the threshold was affectionate and bemused.

How are you? he said. It's nice that I'm finally seeing your place. Don't you think?

Inside, he hung his coat carefully on the communal coat hooks. I thought his expression was a kind of offering. He wanted to show me that he could behave, that he wasn't a monster, now that he had convinced me that I loved his monstrousness. I watched his shoulders relax as he looked around at the kitchen and the living room.

Do you want some tea? I said.

He didn't want tea. I took him into my room, where he kicked off his shoes and lay back on the bed. It's not a bad place, he said.

We like it.

Not like Olivia's.

No, not like Olivia's. I looked at him. How is she?

She's well, Nathan said. She's fine.

I lay down next to him. My room was little, blue-walled, decorated with two mirrors. From the corner of my eye I could see our reflection vaguely—his chest on the bed rising a little above mine. It had seemed obvious to me that Olivia was bound to Nathan even when he hurt her, and here I was, eating out of Nathan's hand.

It's good to see you, he said, without turning toward me.

Did you think you wouldn't?

No. He smiled. No, to be honest, I felt sure I would see you.

Were you waiting for me?

I don't know whether I would say I was waiting. I thought about you. I wondered whether I would hear from you.

Were you angry at me? About last time?

No, Nathan said, with a look of derision. Why should I be angry with you?

I know I can be sort of pushy.

You can, Nathan said. But you know how much I like you.

The feeling I had when Nathan told me that he liked me was unlike anything I had felt before—or it was like falling in love again and again and never growing accustomed to it. In anyone else's mouth it would be mild, inadequate. Yet each time was more shocking than before. All the terms by which I imagined he valued me had been exhausted: My sex no longer surprised him; my body was no longer a novelty. Somehow my beauty was so exquisite that it continued to fascinate him. Or, if it was no longer my beauty that he craved, he had found something in me to admire.

There was a pause in which I thought Nathan could hear my pulse.

I've missed you, he said after a little while. I think we're a bit alike, you and me. Though I don't mean any insult to you by saying so.

He gave a short laugh.

Is that humility, Nathan? I said. I'm shocked.

You aren't shocked. Don't pretend you haven't missed me.

I won't pretend. But do you really think we're alike?

Nathan looked at the ceiling but his hand curled up between us and I felt his fingers lightly on my shoulder. It's a strange thing, he said. Olivia—none of this is natural to her. Sex. I can bring it out in her, but she doesn't know how to move, it's sort of like playing an instrument that's out of tune. It's wonderful to bring her around, but she doesn't have an instinct about it. But you do. You don't just have instinct—you want to investigate it too. You don't just get up and walk away satisfied. You have that absorbing affect—you want to absorb everything. Information, admiration, whatever it is.

I thought you didn't like that, I said. That I asked so many questions.

I'm certainly not as troubled as you are. And I'm trying to free you from your own hang-ups, you know that. But I like that it matters to you. Sex doesn't matter so much to everyone, not in the same way.

Sometimes I think it doesn't matter to any other girl as much as it does to me.

Not many. Nathan smiled again. But you don't need to be miserable about it. Why can't we simply enjoy it? It's a special thing, Eve.

I lay there, my whole being collected into the inch of skin on my shoulder where his fingers rested. My room was small and strange. How was it that I thought of it as my home and believed that it belonged to me? It was just a temporary space that I had hung with things I'd purchased, so that I could believe I was safe inside it. And this was true, too, of everything I had believed about myself: that I was moral, that I was political, that I cared for the realities of strangers who were linked to me by parallel circumstance. These were beliefs I had pinned up so that I could imagine that I belonged to something valuable and that something valuable belonged to me. It was so easy for Nathan to take them down. I wanted to see them fall. I wanted to be brandnew, to experience love and pleasure as though I had never been hurt and never felt fear. And what more could be owed to a woman than that? What more could a woman ask for?

I do enjoy that, I said. I do. I love it.

I know, Nathan said.

But I wish it could be different with Olivia.

What do you wish could be different?

I wish it weren't so hard for her, I said. Can't you see it's hard for her? That she wants more from you than you can give her? She wants you to be her boyfriend, she wants you not to look at anyone else.

That's not true. She enjoys all of this, all our games.

She does, I said. She enjoys your games, because you give them to her and you like them and she likes what you like. But she's heartsick too.

You might be right, Nathan said. There is something that worries me—that she doesn't date anyone else. At first I thought that was fine, that of course she didn't have time or attention for anyone else. But it's been too long now.

I don't see how she could date anyone else. It would be cruel to them. She doesn't have it in her.

That might be true. I've been spending a little less time with her as it is. I'm a little worried about it.

You knew Olivia, you knew her personality, how she felt about you. . . . Weren't you worried about this? How could you imagine she wouldn't make you into her boyfriend and fall madly in love with you?

You don't understand all of it, Nathan said. That's all I can say.

What don't I understand? You think fucking her all the time behind closed doors and refusing to actually date her is confusing or something? You want me to believe she's not in love with you?

She's devoted to me. In her way.

Not everyone is like you, I said. Not everyone can move between different worlds and live like you do. Detached.

You can, Nathan said.

Yes. I think I can. But you know how it is.

I looked at him.

How does it feel? he said.

Most of the time I think it's a curse. Like I'm haunting my own life.

It isn't. That's just misogyny speaking.

You're going to tell *me* what's misogyny now?

Isn't it? That you and I are the same, more than you think, but you're afraid of it, people judge you for it? You're afraid women won't love you because of it? When actually—I mean this, Eve—actually it's a blessing.

But what about Olivia? You know how she feels about you. Why don't you just be with her? Or let her down easy?

You're being narrow-minded.

Come on. This is about Olivia. I worry about her still.

Nathan took his hand from my shoulder and sat up. His face was amused again, not quite legible to me. I was reminded of a look he had given me the first night we met, at Bar Pleiades, where I so often joined them in that first month, a look that told me he enjoyed it when I challenged him.

Do you know what this is? he said. He held up his right hand and showed me his ring. A thick band, domed in the center like a heavy class ring, but without any markings.

No. What is it?

This ring?

So? Are you in some kind of cult?

You really don't know? he said. I felt sure you must have it figured out.

What are you talking about?

I'm married, Eve, Nathan said.

Nathan had been pulling the strings of my life for so long with so little resistance that I couldn't fathom why he should hide anything. In Fatima's eyes I acted with regard to him like a cup that had been emptied and turned on its rim. I sat very still, my whole vision filled by his ring, as though I had never seen one before.

I've been married for seven years, he continued. My wife is Austrian. In Austria they wear the ring on the right hand.

It took me a moment to remember my voice.

But where does she live, I said. In Austria?

No. Nathan laughed. No, she lives in my apartment. With me.

Does anyone know?

Eve, you don't understand. Everyone knows.

Olivia?

Of course. Olivia's known Helen for years. Since college. Truthfully, I thought you'd have figured it out by now.

But what reason would you have to lie to me? I said. Why wouldn't you tell me? I mean, I know about you and Olivia— what was the use—I don't understand. It would have made everything easier. Your terrible schedule, the hotels, the secrecy—

I don't tell anyone I sleep with. Not usually.

I'm not anyone.

No, Nathan said. He reached for my hand and held it. You're right.

Does she know? I said. Your wife?

Of course. But not the details.

Not about Olivia?

Nathan waved a hand in front of his face.

Nathan, I said, I've known you almost a year. You couldn't tell me? After all this, you didn't trust me?

I trust you, he said. I can't explain it easily to you. It's not as though it necessarily makes sense—it's just the way I am. I like to keep things separate, to maintain them in the particular ways in which they need to be maintained. I can't think of Helen when I'm with you, not for more than a moment. It simply doesn't make sense to me. And when I'm with her I never think of you, or Olivia, or anyone else. Not even about work very much. That's just the way that I am. So I don't want to talk to you about her. When I'm with you, that's the last thing on my mind.

Are you really in love? I said. With . . . Helen?

Yes, Nathan said, and he smiled the way he did when I told him about my life with Fatima. That's right. I've been in love with her for ten years.

At his words I felt an expansiveness bloom in my body. I knew his marriage didn't absolve his mistakes at work, I knew it didn't imply he was a good man, and yet his words seemed to release me from a craven vision I'd had: a vision of a man capable of performing feeling but never of inhabiting it. He wasn't dangerous after all—wasn't a sociopath—he had never misled Olivia. He was just in love with a woman I didn't know. I felt overwhelmed with happy luck. For no reason I could think of I imagined him in the driver's seat of a car, looking with mischievous pride at a faceless woman on the passenger side. I had never seen such a human look as I saw on him there, in the car I had drawn in my mind, on a sunny road. I was allowed to love him now. There was space for my love.

Nathan, I said after a moment, this makes me happy. Isn't that strange?

You are very strange. Why does it make you happy?

To find out you go home to love.

He looked at me, still turning the ring around his finger. You like me very much, he said. You didn't, in the beginning, but you do now. That's why I told you.

There's something sad about it too, I said. You're not what I thought you were. Not at all. I thought you floated through things on your own—so independent. I thought you were totally alone, in the end.

I'm just who you think I am. I do float through things on my own. I'm here with you, aren't I?

I was going to ask him how it was that he had managed to have both, but I already knew. Despite how I envied him I felt high, near tears, the way I might at the end of a film or a novel. The proximity of Nathan's life was intoxicating. Our world seemed a landscape of good intentions and possible freedoms. Love seemed to occupy the room with us, as concrete as a body, generous and inextinguishable.

Nathan lay down on the bed again and pulled me into his chest. His shoulder was solid and warm beneath me. His hand gripped mine.

No more secrets, he said after a while. That's all of them.

His revelation was so exquisite that I hoped this wasn't true, that he had some other pot of secrets he was keeping for me, waiting to dole out one after another. But all he said, when he broke the silence, was, Did you get my birthday present?

Oh! Yes, I said. I forgot. Thank you.

When he kissed me I stood to get undressed, and he put a hand out to stop me. Let me take your picture first, he said.

Just like this?

Yes, stand still for a moment.

When he had put his phone down I pulled off my clothes.

You're so beautiful, he said. An ache announced itself in me. His voice was not the voice of the man presiding over the lineup, the voice of the man who had chosen my nude photo from among those posted on the message board. I had never heard this voice before. I felt suddenly that nothing had ever mattered to me so much as this voice.

I held him while he fucked me. The room was black, and there was only the sweat across his shoulders, the grip of his hands underneath me, the sound of his voice in my ear, *That's it, that's it, Eve, do you know, Eve, do you know, do you know, do you know?* I knew.

—

Two months went by this way. Four. Five. The city grew dark. I saw Nathan at irregular intervals, a total of six times over the course of that winter. When I wasn't with him I experienced a new and fickle solitude. Sometimes, when I met people, I felt resigned tenderness toward them: the awareness that they were lonely and seeking a moment of intimacy, just as I was. But this awareness was sour and embarrassing to me. I wanted to be swept into someone else's certainty, to be swept into *something*. In impatience I would try, sometimes, to act as though I was as certain and confident as the person I wished to encounter. For an hour I would look into someone's eyes, refer to my phone every so often with dismissive urgency. At the moment when I wanted the next scene to unfold I would stare into the distance, as though I had already summoned it. *Let's go,* I would say. On a dark, icy evening in Bed-Stuy, I said this to a girl whose quick smile reminded me of Romi's. She was otherwise smaller, more acquiescent, more prone to nervous laughter. She wasn't finished with her drink, but when I finished mine and said, *Let's go,* she gulped hers down and followed me out of the bar. When I fucked her I tried to act as Nathan did: to squeeze my brows together in painful admiration when she revealed her body, to touch her as though she belonged to me and I had done it a hundred times already. *That's the cock for you, isn't it,* I said, my tone so much like Nathan's that for a moment it made me ache. The girl cried out a little, as though she were pushing something out of herself. I felt for her. I thought I could see her loneliness, the way it revolted against a pleasure liable to disappear.

ˋ   I kept my clothes on. I left quickly. The tenderness I felt toward most people—people who were not Nathan—could just as quickly become uneasiness. I had an amorphous feeling around other people, like I was floating in an undifferentiated world. It reminded me of the nightmares I sometimes had in which I forgot how to do basic, obvious things: wandering around a kitchen unable to find the butter, though the butter is always kept in the same place. It seemed to me that drivers did not obey street signs, that the train did not obey its schedule, that all the schemes I had for meaning were slightly twisted. If I spent days alone, on the other hand, it was like the world built itself around me into exactly what I imagined or hoped it was by sheer force of will. One morning as I walked to work I passed a mailbox that was a blinding blue, droplets of leftover rain or some shine catching the sun. *How absolutely gorgeous,* I thought, admiring the mailbox—even among all the superior beauties of the street, the trees, the sky, even the concrete curvature of the block and the ornate façades—not only because it was so bright but because it reminded me what world I was walking through, a world with which I was deeply familiar, where I spoke the language of blue mailboxes, understood their use, and benefited from their service and the systems into which they were incorporated. I felt the web of the city around me: the layers of taxation and bureaucracy that led to the blue mailbox and ensured its continuing daily operation, and all the kinds of letters that had been left in it, the various Brooklyn residents who had utilized it, all the weather it had seen, and the imagined apartments and brownstones and businesses throughout New York and beyond that would receive mail deposited into it. The mailbox gave me a sense of security, as though I was bound inside interlocking structures of such solidity and benevolence that I would be safe as long as I lived. I was conscious of how foolish such a feeling was: that these systems were not solid and that they were not benevolent, that they maintained and reinscribed all the tenets of my world that troubled me even as I benefited from them. And yet I could not shake the instinct I had that I was safe. The pre-invented world promised me that I was already valued and protected, that I did not have to invent value or meaning for my body and my life. Yet around people who were not Nathan—around women most of all—this false security threatened to break down.

I knew just what you wanted, I would hear Nathan's voice saying to me while I waited on a barstool or listened to Fatima talk. Nothing particularly dirty, nothing even genuinely intimate: just the soft hush of certainty. His voice was like a prayer that I kept to myself. *I knew just what you wanted. I knew just what you wanted.* Sometimes, wading through the mess of my emotion, I worried that in Romi's absence I had found nowhere better to put the love I'd felt for her than into Nathan. But then I remembered the safety of Romi—how eager I'd been to become a worthy participant in her world of care and loyalty. There was no comparison between what I had felt for Romi and what I harbored for Nathan. My feeling for Romi had been, more than an extravagance of emotion, an extravagance of aspiration.

I thought often, without restraint, of the moment when Nathan had told me about his wife and the startling flood of feeling that had moved through me. My relationship with him had little resemblance to what I knew as love, contained no safety or certainty or real knowledge. It seemed mistaken to assign love to a person with whom I spent few, anonymous hours, who had never answered the phone when I was in crisis or come, for any reason, when I called. But was I still a person who would deny what I felt simply because I disliked it? That impulse felt broken to me now, childish.

—

Nathan wanted to see me alone. Nathan wanted to see me at my apartment. Nathan wanted to see me for dinner, wanted to take me to the Frick, wanted to meet in the park. We were always alone and it was different than it had been before. What was it that was different? Maybe it was that I could forget for weeks at a time about Olivia—about witnessing and being witnessed—about what it looked like when I sank underneath Nathan. Maybe it was the new gratitude I saw in him. He had given up some portion of his privacy for me, in telling me about his wife, in confiding in me about his life's true landscape, and I could see that in my presence he no longer felt invulnerable. His nonchalance faltered. He acted like a man presented with a feast. His mouth changed shape. He was hard before he undressed. At times it was clear, when he spoke to me, that he was struggling to maintain his composure. He would fidget with his hands. He would say: *You smell so good, you look incredible, does anyone kiss better than you do?* His smooth self-assurance, the sense I sometimes had that he was only performing his duties, was replaced by a hunger I had glimpsed in the way he looked at me but hadn't felt, before, in his touch. He was no longer fully in control—he was not toying with me but satiating himself. When we were together we fucked two, three, four times. When he came it was with a new abandon, a revelation that gripped his whole body, seized his feet, undid his hands, released a roar that engulfed me. I was held completely inside him. His body formed a cup that held me and the cup shook, spilling over with heat and sweat. Afterward we both started to laugh and couldn't stop. Our bodies rippled with laughter. He kissed my forehead. He kissed my collar. He let his hand rest on my belly. God, no one is like you, he said, no one is like you, do you know that? When I said that I was greedy, he said, You are, you're my greedy thing. He kissed me again and again. If I could smell anything for the rest of my life, Eve, he said, it would be you.

———

The next time I saw him it was like that too. It wasn't just the desire—an overwhelming, murderous desire that ate everything it touched, that howled when we saw each other—but the nature of the desire, which lived in absolute solitude and would rather have died than make demands. When I thought of him I didn't text him because it felt good to know that he thought of me too but that we had no need of each other, that we would ask nothing of each other, that what we offered each other was sheer and uncompromised pleasure. When we saw each other he would say, *Every time I come I think of you, every time I come I think of you, every time I come I think of you. It's because you were made to be fucked by me, and I was made to fuck you.*

But what if he were your husband? Fatima said. You wouldn't trust him an inch.

No, no, I wouldn't trust him an inch. But he wasn't my husband. He was the person who liked that I could never be filled, could never get enough, could never say no, could never be pure; he liked that I wanted as much as he did and that it meant as much to me as it meant to him, that I wanted after all that to be alone and free. It was all right—lucky, even—that I was this way and that I was a woman. He could use a partner in crime. He could use a confidante. He could use a girl who would never slow down. He knew that I would do anything for him—that I owed my presence of mind, the comfort I felt in my body, all that I had come to love in myself, to him. It was in this cocoon, in March, that he told me about the lawsuit.

10

I went to see him at the Standard as soon as he asked. It was a Monday, six in the evening. I hadn't shaved but I didn't care: In the beginning it had felt luxuriant and private, the ritual preparation of my body for Nathan and Olivia, the long hours steaming up the bathroom with scented soaps. Now my pride was tied up in showing Nathan glimpses of my real body, my pride that was otherwise so compromised.

He opened the mini-fridge in the hotel sitting room and found us each a beer. When he handed it to me his eyebrows were knit: There was that look of pain, of worship, I spent my whole life waiting on. We sat side by side on the unblemished bed.

Listen, he said. I'm sorry, Eve—you're going to be deposed. Did Olivia tell you about this?

I haven't talked to Olivia in months. What are you talking about?

There's a lawsuit at the office, he said. A woman I interviewed. And they want you to give a deposition.

What did you do?

Nathan smiled. You're so generous toward me, he said.

Nathan.

Nothing, of course.

I recognized it instantly, as in the coin toss, when the quarter landed and I found out what I hadn't known I wanted by the way my heart sank. I was guilty. I had witnessed Nathan's misconduct; I had suspected he was willing to transgress beyond what went on with Olivia; I had willed myself to see what intrigued me and to look away from what alarmed me, because I was a coward. Then I thought: *Perhaps it would feel good to come clean, to be judged. Perhaps it would break the bowl.*

Okay, I said. So you fucked some woman that you interviewed?

You're a little off. But I can't say much more about it.

Nathan. Tell me. You fucked some woman that you interviewed?

Did I say I fucked her? I didn't fuck her.

You didn't?

No. She claims I did and that I promised I would hire her. She's alleging quid pro quo in the interview process.

Did you imply that you would hire her?

Of course not.

And *did* you hire her?

Of course not, of course not.

Nathan, be serious.

Nathan looked at me. Do you really want to know? he said.

What good am I going to be in a deposition? I said finally. Why me?

I was at your apartment the night of. Do you remember? January. This year.

How could I remember—

I came by at eight or nine. You gave me some cheese and crackers—we fucked—your roommate came home at some point, an hour or so later?

I don't know, I said. But I can check our texts.

We'll check them. I was there. And all you need to do is acknowledge that.

Nathan, come on. What if you fucked this girl at seven P.M. and came over to my place at eight? How can I really—

Doesn't matter if I did. Just do this small thing for me. You'll be telling the truth.

With all due respect, Nathan, I think there's probably a lot of fucked-up shit that goes on at your office.

Sure. At any office. But in this instance you're wrong.

Yeah, but you act like it's business as usual! I mean, why shouldn't you end up in some trouble this time?

You know my responsibility is to protect the family, Nathan said. I think you can respect that.

Why can't Olivia help you?

They don't know about my relationship with Olivia.

Nathan looked at me. Our thighs were only a few inches apart, but he didn't touch me. My breath went in and out of my ribs.

Listen, I said, I appreciate that you trust me. I hope you trust me. But, Nathan . . . you have to know how I feel about all this—the fact that you always manage to have it your way. Especially the relationship you have with Olivia. At work.

Nathan continued to look at me with clear, steady eyes. I thought of the day he had visited the café two long winters before, when Romi still picked me up on Sunday evenings in her running shoes, carrying her twin umbrellas. *I'm at work,* I had said to him then. I had tried to be frank, to be cruel, even, so he would know how little he meant to me in my own solid world. His red polo made me want to laugh, but when he spoke to me I knew my own life was simply a blanket that lifted at his touch.

Look, Nathan said. You like to tease me, and I enjoy that about you. But you also have serious integrity. I know you care very much—more than you admit. Olivia is sincere, yes, she cares very much in different ways. But she doesn't share your high-minded ideas. She has a deep loyalty to what she wants and what she has. Morals come into it, of course, and you know we both think our work is very important—Olivia especially, she's sort of a bleeding heart, you can tell—but she's not moralizing on these petty levels. Not between friends. I would say she's governed by loyalty much more than by integrity. If you can understand the distinction I'm making.

So what about my integrity? I said. Don't you think, if I pay attention to my integrity, as you're calling it, then I think essentially you're a criminal?

Not at all. In fact, I'm sure you don't think so.

I would assume that whatever this woman says you did, it's probably true.

I felt a little of my strength come back. It was erotic to challenge Nathan. Yet in the bottom of my mind I knew what was erotic was the knowledge that, in the course of the hours that followed, I would surrender to him.

Don't you agree, Nathan said, that in one sense or another, most people you've fucked were people you shouldn't have fucked? You belonged to someone else, or they did, or there was some inevitable circumstance—an ex's sister, whatever it was. Even me—I know you imagine you shouldn't even fuck *me,* wouldn't you say, given all your beliefs? Nathan smiled. But, he said, I simply did not hurt this woman. I can promise you that. I don't need to elucidate for you all the ways in which this is obviously true.

I'm sure you didn't intend to hurt her, I said.

I didn't intend to, and I didn't.

It doesn't even matter whether you offered her a job or not or whether you implied it—this is the world she lives in, where if she fucks some asshole who interviewed her, she might get hired.

Nathan turned sideways on the bed to face me and put his hand on my waist. His body was slowly growing softer, but because he was still young there was a boyishness to the gentle pockets of fat on his torso and his hips. He had started going to the gym and I remembered that Olivia had teased him about it once. But she enjoyed the new strength in his shoulders.

Where's Olivia? I asked.

She's not here plenty of the time. Haven't we been seeing each other this way? Just the two of us?

How am I going to give a deposition, I said, if no one knows about you and Olivia? I mean, I can't say anything about you or our relationship without mentioning her.

Nathan found his glasses on the nightstand and put them on.

Of course you can, he said. You can tell the truth. We met online. We've been seeing each other for about a year and a half. I've never deceived you. You know about my marriage and my wife knows about you. I often visit you at your apartment, where I was that evening. There's no need to mention Olivia.

You're kidding.

Listen to yourself. You'd think you were a real believer in the justice system. Is that what you think? You believe justice is going to be granted to this woman? That justice will be meted out at my expense? And that it will be deserved?

I don't have any idea what justice will be done or not, but it won't be mine, will it? So why—

What justice would be yours, Eve? What justice are you looking for? Do you feel you've suffered some injustice? Are you about to sue me too?

Of course not.

What, then?

I don't want anything, I said finally. You know that, Nathan.

Okay, then. The fact is, he said, and I'm sorry to say this, but you will be deposed whether or not it suits you. I wish it weren't the case. I'm not interested in involving you in anything so sordid. Circumstances are beyond me at this point. The question is simply whether or not you'll be my friend here.

Nathan leaned forward again, resting his elbow on his knee, as though in supplication or disappointment. Neither of these were attitudes I had ever glimpsed in him. When we were alone like this I wanted him to be worthy of a doubtless, earnest friendship. Yet it felt so meager—that this was what it was to be his friend.

Eve, he said. Let's be straight with each other. You can cut this act that you don't like me—just for the moment. We both know I enjoy that act, all right? But let's be clear. You've been seeing me for a long time now. You know that I come right up to the line but that I don't cross it. Sometimes I ask you whether you like how I treat you, but I know that you do, and I know that you also like to be asked, which is why I ask you. I've always respected what you wanted—not just respected it but intuited it, discovered it, given it to you, in fact. Isn't that true?

Yes.

You know Olivia and me well, Nathan said. You've known us almost since she and I began seeing each other—not long after. I know you've always had some issues with our work, that you don't like that we fuck because of the fact that Olivia works for me, but you can see that I treat Olivia very well. We have a mutual agreement about our relationship. Olivia understands the terms of my marriage and respects it. And Olivia, she would be a mess without me—she gets tied up in knots, she's very anxious, and I'm the one who settles her, who helps her out of a rut. I create this whole little world that she uses to paint, to be inspired. I work through her new ideas with her. You're going to her show in a couple of months, I assume. She has something she wanted for a long time. Isn't that true?

Yes.

We might have our differences, Nathan said, but it's obvious that in some significant sense you respect me, or you wouldn't be so eager for me to fuck you all the time. You like a little rough play, a little sense that I can fuck the shit out of you and that I absolutely will, but I always ask you if you want it and you always say yes. You trust me. You know that what I care about is not hurting anyone or anything so petty. Do you really think I should be treated as a criminal? That I would assault some woman who came into the office, that I would stoop that low, that real coercion has anything to do with how I seduce women?

I looked at him closely. I knew his body and it was unthreatening to me now, with its new vulnerability, the familiar weight of his hand. If he had frightened me, had it not been a fright my mind and heart required in order to learn to live with the integrity he spoke of?

He kissed me and I saw him once again on that sunny road that the revelation of his marriage had created in me, his collar open, his face full of joy.

Nathan, of course not, I said.

I know, he said. He smiled again. So you'll tell that to the attorneys. And, listen—you can tell the truth. But if you want the advice of a natural liar, all you need to know is, don't lie. Say, *You're close, but you're wrong.* Say you can't explain it. Just gesture at the truth without confirming it.

I recognized in this advice Nathan's whole orientation toward life, narrowed to a point—how he managed his wife, Olivia, me, and God knew what else. The way he maintained what he felt was his integrity while preserving his freedom.

And, don't worry, you'll have my lawyers, of course, Nathan added.

I won't. I'll handle that. Don't you think I should have my own lawyer?

Whatever you'd like.

Nathan, I said, how can you be all right about this?

There will be a settlement, he said. It's just a nuisance.

—

It isn't you that's on trial, Fatima said. Say whatever you want.

There's no trial. Not yet. And hopefully there won't be one.

Why shouldn't there be? Fatima said. We were in our kitchen, lounging against the counters. I hope it goes to trial, she said, and I hope that woman gets her due. Just tell the truth. He deserves it.

You think that?

Well, to the extent that anyone deserves to be legally censured. But yeah. I mean, does this woman deserve a payout because he fucked with her? And should you help her get it? Of course, she said, pulling the kettle off its base, and you're in a unique position to do it. He's trusting you here.

But that's the whole point. He's trusting me here. I can't betray that.

Oh, really? You can't betray his trust? Fatima looked at me in mock surprise, holding the kettle aloft over the counter. Anytime you want, you can forsake this dinner party and jump into real life!

Come on, Fati.

What? Isn't it time you left the fucking dinner party and got real?

It's not like that. Yes, he's a private person. So he hasn't always been forthcoming with me—so what? He hasn't done anything wrong, not to me. I wanted what he gave me. He didn't hurt me.

What about how he *lied* about being *married*? For almost a year?

So what? He's not my boyfriend. And, you know what, I'm happy he's married—I always thought he was just stringing Olivia along for fun, and you know how much that bothered me. But it turns out she knew from the beginning.

Jesus Christ, Eve. What you're saying, essentially, is: *I found out the man I've been fucking had been lying to me about being married for, what, a year, and I'm so relieved he's not a sociopath—*which, by the way, he may well be—*so glad he's happily married!* Do you have any idea how I would react to something like this? To being lied to and manipulated like this? You love to be manipulated by him!

So what if I do? I said. I spilled the mug Fatima had given me. I do! If this is what manipulation is—I love it.

What do you love? The way he sneaks around with that girl? Fucks you on the side? Lies to his wife—

She knows—

You have no idea if she knows! What makes you think he's some great husband? That she has any idea he's fucking other people? Or that you can believe anything he tells you?

He's not a bad person, Fati. He's not.

Are you this blind? The dick is *that* good?

How can I think he's a bad person? I said. When he's the only person who will actually face how I feel—talk to me about it—never judge me for it—understand it—love me for it, even?

You think he loves you?

I'm not saying I think he's good. I don't know what he does with other girls—I don't know. But with me and Olivia, it's not what I thought. I trust that he cares about us. He's just more honest than other people. Less inhibited. He's not afraid of things the way we are.

Damn straight, Fatima said, he's never had to fear a single fucking thing! You act like you have to help him here, but we both know he's going to get away with it whether you help him or not. Why do you think I don't like him, Eve? I'm uncomfortable with people like this—these white people who don't ever have to face any consequences. Fatima gripped the counter behind her, her knuckles taut. I know you want to be like him, she said, and I know how all this seems to you. You look like them, you talk like them, it feels like you can be like them, doesn't it. Living with no regard for the rules. But you can't. Do you know that? You don't want to hurt people. You can't be like him! You can't have those things!

Don't you think I interrogate myself about this? Don't you know I've beaten myself up over this for months and months? I hate myself for having fucked him even once, let alone for liking it this much. I *know* all this! Why are you putting me through this?

I love you, Fatima said, her tone softening. I want you to be safe, and I don't want you to be gaslit all the time. I want people to respect you! For you to be able to rely on them! I'm not the one putting you through something. I love you, Eve, that's all. This is called love.

I felt heartbroken then. It was Fatima I would betray by helping Nathan, earnest, determined Fatima, Fatima who harbored none of my weaknesses, simply because she hoped for more from women than this blind loyalty. It was her definition of love that was the more complete; her love was a resolution to protect me and to sanctify the world. It made me ashamed to call what I felt for Nathan love—that scarce, heady pleasure and gratitude which could turn, in the next minute, to indignation. I filled the tea mug again and sat down.

Regardless, I said, I need a lawyer.

Right. Fatima looked at me. I can ask my grandfather. Maybe he or one of his colleagues can take it on.

It was painful to me to receive this offer. I knew it was made out of care and yet it seemed to confirm my weakness, my ineptitude—that I needed help could only mean that Fatima was right. I couldn't be like Nathan. I wasn't like him. However often I had believed it, I was not alone and sovereign, floating through a vast world of infinite freedoms.

Fati, I don't want to bring your grandfather into this. I don't want anyone in your family to know about it.

What, then?

I'll ask my father. I don't think there's much choice.

For money?

Well, no. I don't want him to know about the deposition either. But I think I can just . . . I don't know . . . I think I can sort of get something out of him.

Okay, Fatima said.

I mean that I think he wants to help me, I said. He wants to help me, but I make it difficult. I hurt his pride. So then he makes the money disappear—you know, pretends that I'm on my own. And I like pretending that I'm on my own too. But I think, if I wanted . . . you know.

Eve, Fatima said, did Nathan offer you a lawyer? Because you shouldn't have to deal with this at all.

He did. But don't you think . . . I don't know.

Fatima looked at me kindly. I thought this was the first time, in all our conversations about Nathan, that she understood my feelings. Okay, she said. I think you're right. At least you can have your own lawyer. We'll call your father tomorrow.

—

I sat on the stoop in the morning to call him. It was still winter, and there was a clear, desolate feeling on the street, a sense of brutal reality. The only other people outside were hurrying toward the subway, faces hidden below wool hats. I lit a cigarette and let it burn three-quarters of the way down before I pressed his name.

He picked up after two rings.

Evie, he said. Are you calling me on purpose?

Yeah, Dad. I'm calling you on purpose.

What a surprise, he said, with a half-amused tone that I knew was hiding hurt.

How are you?

Fine. Fine, as always.

Good, I said. Good.

And what about you? How's work going?

Oh, I'm starting a new job, actually. In a few weeks.

My father whistled. I could hear his shameless joy through the phone. Then he paused.

What kind of job? he said.

A real one. At an office.

At an office?

Yeah. It's called a family office. It's sort of like an investment firm. They handle everything for one family—their estate, financials, that kind of thing.

A family office. Really.

Yeah. You know, as a consultant.

Do they know who they're hiring?

Shut up, Dad, I said, listening to him laugh. I'm smart, aren't I?

Well, that's wonderful, Evie, he said. That's just great. I'm really proud of you.

Health insurance and everything.

You deserve it.

Thanks, I said. And I actually—the thing is, I actually found this job through a guy I've been seeing. He's higher up there.

Aha, my father said. Nothing untoward, I hope? Since you'll be starting there soon?

I recognized in his voice a grudging, jocular excitement for gossip. I used the same tone. I tried to laugh it off.

No, I said. Nothing untoward. Different department. But he's been very sweet and helpful.

Really, my father said. That's amazing, Evie. What's his name? Where did you meet him?

His name's Nathan, I said. But listen, Dad, I don't want to— It's so new, I don't want to jinx it. And things are going to be a bit odd as it is starting a new job in the same building. Can we, you know, can we table it for a while?

Nathan, my father said. Of course. Yes. I'll look forward to hearing more about it. But he's . . . he's a serious guy?

Very serious.

Good for you.

And does he—

Dad, I said. Tabling it.

Right, right, my father said. Okay. Listen, I know it's already almost time for the next one—it just flies by—but I never got a chance to give you that gift for your birthday. Last summer.

Oh, right. I forgot.

I know, my dad said. You're my self-sufficient girl, aren't you.

I laughed.

No, seriously, my father said. Listen, it's just a silly thing, but I got you something a little special. If you don't want it I can give it to one of Jeff's kids. It's no problem. I just thought, you know, it might make traveling a bit easier. Coming to visit—or, I don't know, whatever you want. The beach. Upstate. Whatever.

What is it?

It's just a little car. A Volvo. Not that little. But, you know, not a huge deal.

Dad, that's very generous.

It's not new.

Dad, that doesn't matter, that's very generous of you. Has it been sitting in your garage? All these months?

Well, I take it out for a spin every so often. Keep it from falling apart, you know.

Oh, is it about to fall apart?

My father laughed. No, Evie, no, he said. I actually think you'll like it.

The intrusion of childhood, of childishness, made me nauseous and claustrophobic. I remembered this vividly: owing gratitude to someone for whom I represented a kind of error to be corrected. Nathan had expanded my sense of what my adulthood could contain, but now I remembered it could be taken from me again in the span of a half hour. I knew that if I saw Nathan anytime soon I would smack him for bringing me to this place.

All right, I said. Well, that's very sweet of you.

I can ship it down to you, he said, if you don't have the time to come visit right away. With the title and everything.

In a hurry to get it out of the way, huh?

Just eager to celebrate your birthday, and your new job, he said, with a soft smile in his voice that made me shut my eyes with shame. I'm glad you'll have it, finally.

Thanks, Dad. It's really generous of you.

You deserve it.

Sure. Although what is *deserving*, anyway?

That sounds more like my girl. Give it a rest. I'll arrange the shipping tomorrow.

Thanks, Dad.

I hung up and lit another cigarette. After ten minutes or so Fatima poked her head out onto the stoop.

What happened? she said.

Don't you think Nathan could've been a little less stupid? I said. God, I mean, he has all the goddamn pussy he needs. He doesn't need this bullshit.

You don't need this bullshit, you mean.

Yeah, okay, *I* don't need this bullshit. It's so easily avoidable! Why does he have to shit where he eats?

Not like it's the first time.

I grimaced and gestured lamely with the cigarette pack.

So I take it it didn't go well, Fatima said.

No, actually. It went great.

It did?

It went so well that I'm honestly rethinking the whole thing. Feels like a trap.

It's not a trap, Fatima said. It's your *father*. You're starting to lose it, Eve.

Not like it's a trap *he's* going to catch me in. Just that it feels too easy. You know—if I had to fight it out, I'd think he was an asshole and I sort of deserved to get whatever I needed out of him.

He *is* an asshole, Fatima said, shivering, the door still half open. And he doesn't need all that money. I mean, what can one person need with hundreds of thousands of dollars a year?

I can't believe *now* you're in favor of lying.

I didn't say anything about lying. Did you have to lie?

He's giving me a car. And obviously I'm going to sell it.

Not a lie, Fatima said. Just a necessary disappointment.

I beckoned Fatima out for a cigarette. She kept the door open a crack, wrapped her left arm around herself.

Sometimes I can't believe I've kept on seeing Nathan for so long, knowing he's like this, I said. I know I defend it with you. I feel like I have to. But I can't really justify it either.

Fatima looked soft. She put a hand on my shoulder and leaned down to dip a cigarette into the flame I held out for her. Do you remember what Eve says? she said. Babitz? About sex masterpieces?

I love that phrase, I said. Sex masterpieces.

How we should recognize them for the creative adventures they are, she said, with a reluctant smile. Our love scenes. The only chance we'll ever get to touch the face of heaven.

———

The following week I went to Nathan's office to speak to his lawyers. The office was downtown, twenty floors above a broad marbled lobby where men who looked like Nathan moved through revolving doors. Did I love them too? Was I that shallow? Or was Nathan's suit merely a costume that I had torn from him? The scenery made me unsympathetic. I was wearing the gold jewelry I had inherited from my mother—all my rings, two heavy bracelets—and a pencil skirt I had bought for a job interview years earlier. I showed my ID at the main desk and a secretary met me outside the elevator bank. I waited a long time on a cushioned bench, pulling a clementine from my bag and slowly peeling it apart.

The conference room was filled with the delicate noise of glass, the scent of a mild antiseptic. Beneath it I could smell my own faint sweat. In the room were two lawyers. One of them, middle-aged, with a permanently skeptical expression, remained silent throughout the entire meeting. The other was young and heavy-jawed, wearing a suit cut too slim. He thanked me for coming in and introduced himself as Mr. Mora.

He asked me a short series of preliminary questions. The night they were interested in was January 14.

Yes, I said, it's true. I was with Nathan that night. We have some texts from around six P.M. where he agrees to come over. And I saw him not long after that.

And do you know what time he arrived?

I can't be sure. But as far as I can remember, not long after I had dinner. Maybe around eight or so.

To the best of your memory, you were with Mr. Gallagher at eight P.M. on the evening of January 14?

Yes.

And did he mention Ms. Sabitova to you at all that evening?

No.

All right. Mr. Mora smiled. That's great, he said. Listen, Ms. Cook, we're very pleased to have you here, and what you have to say is very helpful. And the fact is that we fully expect this all to be settled privately. But we want you to be aware that it's likely that during discovery Ms. Sabitova's lawyers will be interested in your relationship with Mr. Gallagher, and it might be a little uncomfortable for you. I understand, I said. Uncomfortable?

Well, obviously they'll want to know how you met Mr. Gallagher, how long your relationship has been going on, what it looks like. These are things Mr. Gallagher and you yourself have already told us. And, as you know, your relationship with Mr. Gallagher is extramarital. So it's possible they will be interested in questioning your trustworthiness on this front. Just as they are interested in discrediting Mr. Gallagher's trustworthiness. But Mr. Gallagher tells us that you're a close friend of his and that there's no need for us to worry that you would incriminate him. In terms of his character.

No, I said. That's true.

So just to confirm, Ms. Cook: Your relationship with Mr. Gallagher has been entirely consensual?

Yes.

And you trust and respect him?

Of course.

Have you ever seen Mr. Gallagher coerce or assault anyone, including yourself, or approach any woman without consent?

No.

Would you believe him capable of it?

No.

Has Mr. Gallagher ever spoken to you in any detail about anything related to his work?

No.

Has he ever offered you any kind of position or compensation or implied that such a thing might be possible in the future?

No.

How has Mr. Gallagher treated you, in general?

Very well, I said. He's very attentive. An excellent listener.

We've noticed that too, Mr. Mora said. He smiled again. And how do you feel about women? And the climate generally?

Excuse me?

The political climate, he said. With regard to women and lawsuits such as this one.

Mr. Mora had thick, perfectly groomed brows which I was hesitant to believe weren't helped by waxing or pomade.

I think it's a real shame that women are in this position, I said.

Would you clarify that for us?

I'm a people pleaser, I said. I try hard to get people to like me. I take it that's what you want me to do.

Don't you want to help Mr. Gallagher?

Yes. I care a lot about Nathan. I don't want to see him go through this.

Mr. Mora didn't look pleased. But it seemed that they couldn't do without me, certainly not now.

And with regard to Ms. Olivia Weil, he said. We don't have any reason to believe that Ms. Sabitova's attorneys know anything about Ms. Weil. But, just to be clear, does everything you've said with regard to Mr. Gallagher apply to his relationship with Ms. Weil as well?

I was surprised, though perhaps I shouldn't have been. I had to have known somewhere that Nathan was not so powerful as he imagined. Nathan's lawyer looked away graciously while I paused.

Yes, I said. Everything I said is true. I don't know anything about Nathan mistreating Olivia, which is what you're asking, I think.

There will be no need to mention Ms. Weil, unless she is referenced explicitly by Ms. Sabitova's attorneys, Mr. Mora reminded me. Which we don't expect her to be. Obviously.

—

When I walked out of the lobby onto the street I called my father. He answered right away.

I lied, Dad, I said. I didn't get a job. And I don't want a new job. Or at least not what you're calling a "real" one. I just don't want you to give so many shits about it one way or another. What does it matter? If I'm not coming to you begging for handouts?

There was a pause during which I heard only the wind and the shudder of a train passing underground. The skin of my hands felt raw. I pushed my left hand into my coat pocket.

All right, my father said. Fine. And the stuff about your new man? Nathan?

Also a lie.

Another pause, a sigh. Or maybe my father was outside too—maybe it was the brush of wind against his phone.

But you're not still with Romi? he said.

Don't mention Romi to me ever again, okay?

But you're still a lesbian?

You can keep the car. If you've already shipped it I'll send it back.

You can keep it, Evie, he said. I don't need it. And I'd still like you to come and visit, you know. When you have the time.

I said goodbye, hung up, called Nathan before I could lose my nerve. I had never called him before. It made me feel briefly new and naïve again—as though I was in danger of overreaching.

Eve, Nathan said. Is everything okay?

You call me for no reason. Except to bother me. Can't I call you for no reason?

Sure, Nathan said, a familiar grin in his voice. I thought I heard the ambiguous click of a door or maybe a bottle. Probably he was at work, just twenty stories above me. Yes, he said, I'm happy to hear your voice.

I'm going to take you up on that offer to pay for the lawyers, I said. This is your mess. I don't want to pay for it.

That's exactly right. Of course. Don't worry about it.

I've decided that I can't possibly escape complicity with you. And the idea that I could somehow be impartial or something if I just had an independent lawyer seems like a delusion.

You're not complicit, Nathan said. There's been no wrong-doing.

Just so you know, I'm pissed at you.

Are you really?

I turned around on my heel on the sidewalk, leaning first the right side of my body and then the left against the cold stone façade. Nathan was quiet. Still grinning, I imagined.

No, I said. Not really. But fuck you.

I really am sorry about all this, Nathan said. I miss you, you know.

———

It was Mr. Mora who accompanied me to the offices of the attorneys on West 33rd. He told me that the deposition would likely last only an afternoon, though they might stretch it to two days at most. There was a definite wariness between us that reminded me of the mood in the first months Nathan and I were seeing each other. Mr. Mora was more formal than Nathan but treated me with the same familiar amusement that threatened to devolve into condescension were I to reveal myself to be stupid rather than difficult. Nevertheless I found him a comforting presence when we were settled into a dark, narrow meeting room with the opposing attorneys. I felt as though condescension might be valuable under these circumstances.

The cuticle on my right thumb had begun to bleed by the time Ms. Sabitova's attorney said, How long have you known Mr. Gallagher?

She wore graying curls and had a voice like a customer-service representative. Though she wasn't smiling, her tone implied that she knew basic politeness would go a long way.

About a year and a half, I said.

How did you meet?

Online.

How and when?

On a message board. In December, not this past December but the year before. I don't remember the exact date. He responded to a post I made.

What was the post about?

Is that relevant?

It's not relevant, Mr. Mora said. Ms. Bullens?

All right. So you had known each other just over a year at the time when Mr. Gallagher came to see you on January 14?

Yes.

What time did he arrive?

Around eight P.M.

Do you remember this precisely?

We texted earlier that evening about when he would come over. I remember that I had dinner alone at home and he arrived not long afterward. So I think it must have been not much later than eight. Though obviously I didn't write down the time.

Do you live alone, Ms. Cook?

No. I have a roommate.

Was your roommate home at the time?

She wasn't home when Nathan came over, but she was there later on in the evening. She and Nathan saw each other when he left, I think.

And did Mr. Gallagher mention Ms. Sabitova to you that evening?

No.

Did you discuss his work or the hiring process in any way?

I don't remember, I said. I don't think so.

You don't think so?

We almost never discuss his work.

All right, said Ms. Bullens. She pushed a gray lock back from her temple. I'm just going to ask some questions about your relationship with Mr. Gallagher. How soon after meeting him did your relationship become romantic?

I wouldn't say it's romantic.

Excuse me. How soon after meeting him did your relationship become sexual?

The night we met.

Why did you choose to begin a sexual relationship with him?

I had a feeling I would like being with him. The same way you make any decision.

Do you regularly make decisions based on feelings?

I don't know, I said. Not always. Sometimes.

Did you know at the time that Mr. Gallagher was married?

No.

Would you say that he took pains to conceal his marriage from you? That he hid his ring or made any other attempts to conceal it from you?

No. I don't think so.

He simply didn't mention it?

He didn't mention it.

Don't you think that's something a person is obligated to mention in a sexual situation?

Ms. Cook, Mr. Mora said, you don't have to answer that.

I don't think there are absolute rules, I said. I had a girlfriend when we met. And I didn't tell Nathan about my girlfriend either.

Beside me, Mr. Mora ran a hand along his jaw. Ms. Bullens smiled mildly.

Okay, Ms. Bullens said. How would you characterize your relationship with Mr. Gallagher? After your first meeting, how often did you see each other?

It varied a lot. We saw each other maybe once a month, sometimes more, sometimes less.

And what were your meetings like?

We usually spent three or four hours together. We talked.

What did you talk about?

My life, usually, I said. Different things I was thinking about. Especially about sexuality, ideas, that kind of thing.

Was it a consensual relationship?

Of course.

Were you hoping for any kind of professional or monetary assistance from him?

No.

Did you ever receive any?

No.

And when did you find out Mr. Gallagher was married?

About six months ago.

How did you find out?

He told me.

Why do you think he told you?

We're intimate. He told me as a friend.

Did your relationship change at that point?

What do you mean?

Did it end?

No.

Did you ever feel in any way coerced by Mr. Gallagher?

No.

Did you ever find him aggressive?

I wished suddenly that Nathan were in the room. I could see him as he was in the hotel suite again, leaning forward, his elbow resting on his knee, his eyes convincingly soft. When he spoke to me about the lawsuit, was he concealing his fear or was he scrupulously convinced of his own innocence? I thought the second—not that he was convinced of his innocence in any legal or moral paradigm, but that he believed himself exempt.

I never felt unsafe around him, I said.

Did you find him aggressive, Ms. Cook?

Sometimes he could be dominant, sexually. But the dynamic was consensual. He always asked permission.

Did you feel powerless in your relationship with him?

It depends on what you mean—I guess. By powerless.

Did you ever feel manipulated by Mr. Gallagher?

I wanted more than anything to be capable of perfect sincerity. But what could I say? Not one day had passed since I'd met Nathan that I did not feel in some way under his thumb, yet I chose him again and again; it was a manipulation that sated me, one in which I participated. If I had left him behind, he would have let me go wordlessly, I had never doubted it.

To be honest, I said, I did sometimes feel manipulated by him. He's very charming. But I signed on to the relationship that we had. I liked being treated the way he treated me, and I told him that.

The attorney paused and looked down at a note card in her hand. She pushed her glasses up her nose.

I've always been confident that if I ever wanted Nathan to stop, in any way, he would, I said.

Was Ms. Olivia Weil ever a part of your sexual relationship?

I looked at Mr. Mora. His expression was blank.

Yes, I said. Sometimes.

How often?

I don't know.

Was she with you more or less than half the time, when you met?

Less.

Was she with you on the night of January 14?

No.

Why not?

I don't know. It wasn't unusual. I didn't ask.

Would you say you were close to her?

No.

Did you understand that Ms. Weil and Mr. Gallagher worked together?

Yes.

How much did you understand about Mr. Gallagher's relationship with Ms. Weil at work?

Not much. They were very private about work.

And what did you think about their illicit working relationship?

I was concerned about her.

Why were you concerned about her?

She can seem like a timid person. Sensitive.

Were you concerned that Mr. Gallagher would take advantage of her?

Not really. It's not really that I thought Nathan would take advantage of her . . . it's more that it just felt very important. You know, in the case that they were to break up or something were to happen, work would become difficult for them both. For her especially. I never thought that Nathan would punish her at work or anything like that.

Were you aware that their relationship was against company policy and that it was clandestine?

Yes.

And this did not give you pause?

It did.

Why did you continue to see Mr. Gallagher and Ms. Weil, in that case?

I liked them both, I said. They were exciting.

Was it easy for you to put aside your concerns?

It wasn't. No. But I didn't want to be unfairly judgmental. Things seemed to be working for them . . . and what do I know about how other people should live? They were happy. I tried to let Olivia know that I . . . that I was available for her. If she needed anything.

If she needed anything?

Help, support, whatever. If she wanted to talk about him, or anything.

Did she ever reach out to you for support?

No.

Why not?

I don't know. You'd have to ask her.

You mentioned that you and Mr. Gallagher would sometimes discuss ideas and sexuality, she said. What kind of ideas did you discuss?

Different things.

Can you clarify?

This was over the course of a year. Longer. So obviously I don't remember all of it.

Did you share the same ideas?

In general.

Were there any important differences?

Sometimes we disagreed, I said. Sure. In a friendly way.

Did you have a problem with any of Mr. Gallagher's personal or political positions?

Sometimes. Of course.

Can you elaborate?

I looked at Mr. Mora for help.

It's too broad a question, unfortunately, Ms. Bullens, he said. Ms. Cook can't answer that.

Did any of Mr. Gallagher's positions strike you as unusual or threatening?

No.

Did you disagree on the topic of sexuality?

I don't know what you mean.

Did the two of you have the same ideas about how sexuality works and what constitutes it?

No, not always.

Did it trouble Mr. Gallagher that you were not heterosexual?

I don't see why it would, I said. No. It didn't.

If you don't mind, Ms. Bullens said, why was it that you began a relationship with Mr. Gallagher, given that you had a girl-friend at the time?

I can't really answer that. I don't know.

A choice made based on a feeling, then?

Yes.

Ms. Bullens paused briefly and looked into her hands, as though cradling something delicate, something that pained her. When she raised her head there was a change in her voice. No longer solicitous, it was the voice of a teacher or a parent, gentle and condescending, full of superior knowledge.

Would you call yourself a feminist? she said finally.

Yes.

And what does that mean to you?

I looked at Ms. Bullens. If I saw her on the street or exiting a subway car, there would be something to admire in her; she had a steeliness I liked, a straight-backed, no-nonsense look. She managed to make her business attire look vaguely her own with the addition of sharp old-fashioned glasses. And how could I not respect her for representing women like Nathan's Ms. Sabitova, a name I could picture only as a blond wound? But I couldn't really believe that she was asking this of me. If she would support Ms. Sabitova, there was no good reason, no adequate reason in the world, why she would not support me too—or at least hear me in good faith. Instead, she, who more likely than not felt herself responsible for some great part of the sacrifices and leadership that had resulted in the landscape of freedoms I enjoyed, was devoting herself to a project that seemed to me, despite all my admitted mistakes, despicable. My relationship with Nathan made me promiscuous, my decision to sleep with him made me thoughtless, my willingness to trust him made me stupid, my bisexuality made me inconsistent, and now my feminism was going to make me treacherous.

That's not an easy question, I said. Respectfully.

Please try to describe what it means to you.

Feminism, I said. Okay. It means an awareness of difference and an awareness of its social effects. Conscious and unconscious, personal and systemic. A commitment to this awareness and to acting in accordance with it. Toward justice. That's a poor working definition, I'm sorry.

Not equality, the attorney asked, her brow raised, but justice?

I think equality has become an empty word recently.

Would you not say that Mr. Gallagher has an awareness of what you call this difference, and its effects, and that he has acted in accordance with it, not in the service of justice but instead to further his own interests? Has he not done that with both you and Ms. Weil, to your knowledge?

He's made me very happy, I said. Both me and Olivia. His awareness of difference, as you're calling it—it's served me as much as it's served him. Maybe even more.

The attorney leaned back and opened her hands. I felt despair and its new, strange twin, an anger I couldn't yet explain, an anger not at myself but at the mysterious source of my conviction that what most fulfilled me could only be suspect. To whom was I responsible? To Ms. Bullens and Ms. Sabitova? To queer women? To the dream of justice? To myself? To Olivia?

Unfortunately, the attorney said, however you might justify Mr. Gallagher's actions toward yourself and Ms. Weil, they have not served my client, and they have certainly not been made in the service of any kind of justice.

—

On the night we met, after he had fucked me for the first time, I asked Nathan how he had known that I wanted to sleep with him. I didn't think that I would see him again, and I was especially curious because I still didn't know how or when, in the three hours I had spent in his company, I had made the decision myself.

Nathan poured some wine and smiled. He said, While we were outside at the bar having a smoke, I complimented your shoes. When you give a compliment there are no false positives. Sometimes a woman will respond demurely, or unhappily, and usually that's a lack of interest, though there can sometimes be a false negative. But there aren't any false positives. What I mean by a positive is not that she accepts the compliment but that it really lands. When she responds, you can see that it meant something to her. That she doesn't brush it off, that she's delighted.

And how did I respond? When you complimented my shoes? You were delighted. You remember.

When I raised my wineglass I felt at the first touch of the glass to my mouth the awareness that this warm, strict body was *the* reality of glass—this was what glass was, and I was perceiving it—and I felt viscerally around me the sofa and the side table, the cotton of the shirt I had shrugged on, the embossed doors and ceramic lamps and the cabs hustling by in the dark and the new slush beneath their wheels, the glass of the windshields, the grass in the park. I felt that I knew exactly what constituted every material and characterized the life inside it, and I was madly humbled by the vastness and the wonder of my certainty, a blunted version of which I had felt two decades earlier while sitting beside my father in a church pew. I could see it all from above, like a pearly, singing map.

I had always thought that freedom was the power to understand what I could and live by it—to talk myself into things. It seemed to me now that freedom was the strength and the space to follow what moved me. What I had to reconcile myself to was being subject to my emotion, which I would always be striving to comprehend. *What better way could there be to live? To be in constant motion toward something perfect, a motion that would carry you to the end of your life?*

———

I thought of my father as I left the conference room and emerged into a prematurely dusky, blunt day. The new spring trees were bowing in a gray wind, a smell in the air of turned earth.

Throughout my adulthood I had thought often about what my father had said—that women were the easier choice—and in the shadow of Nathan I had begun to think perhaps it wasn't true that women were the easier choice but that I would always make whatever choice was easier. Perhaps my father had been able to see that I was weak. I remembered Olivia's eyes and the way it had felt in my gut to wonder, as I lay naked and uncertain, what it was she needed and how I would ever provide it. I had dreamed that because I was a woman maybe I could be essential or good to her in a way Nathan could not.

I walked down into the belly of the subway and stood waiting on the platform. There was something missing, and all of us knew that, all of us at least on our lucky streets that bloomed in the summer, the ones that we had done little to deserve—some belief in a genuine world, access to a feeling beyond flirtation and ambition. And it was this genuine world that I had wanted Olivia and me to see in each other. I had wanted this even though I worried that what I was doing with Nathan and Olivia was trifling—was flirtation and ambition. And Romi: Romi was the genuine world. Romi had made me feel that it was possible to know people like Darcy and Edmund Bertram, straight out of the paperbacks Olivia and I both enjoyed, and to believe in them at the expense of everyone else, to jettison all the half-assing, the climbing and self-delusion. Romi was a person who gave requisite thought to serious matters. A person whose love was constant and given only where it was earned. Or so I had believed. But I was also afraid to become a serious person, as Romi was, because people were seldom loved in our world, in our century of self-interest and conditional love, for their sincerity or their steadfastness. These were qualities we associated with old men whom we no longer admired. If we loved the image of Darcy, with stoic dignity, making an anonymous sacrifice for love of Elizabeth, what would we think of his qualities in a man we knew personally—his reticence, his condescension and judgment? Steadfastness and sincerity were religious qualities—terms for how one might prioritize others over oneself. How one might respect other people as sacred, their realities as sacred and not to be trifled with. We knew we ourselves were sacred and since there was no one else to protect us we would protect ourselves by becoming the triflers, to prevent being subject to them. Would it be easier if we felt ourselves protected by some other code of conduct—the belief that others would be shamed for trifling, that trifling was an indication of a weak character, of some essential lack of respect? Were we or were we not to hold ourselves responsible for treating people as though they existed only to entertain us and fulfill our wishes? We could not treat people this way, we knew it. And yet we also could not live as though we were selfless, as though we had the same beliefs about ourselves as those old men did. There was an unkindness in living that way: an unkindness in setting sincerity and steadfastness against a backdrop of characters who could only be, by comparison, thoughtless, petty, cruel. Nathan recognized this intuitively. I had chosen to treat Nathan as something more than a trifle—to treat him as real—because he had given my trifling life, in all its greed and flirtatiousness and secrecy, its absolute reality. And he had shown me that it was possible to have a life like ours, full of trifles and nevertheless sincere and steadfast.

I climbed out of the subway in Clinton Hill and walked to Olivia's apartment. Then, remembering that she would not yet be home from work, I bought a pack of cigarettes on her corner and smoked them while I waited. I didn't know what I should say to her and I felt as though I never would.

—

I woke to Olivia's hand gentle on my cheek. I recognized the gesture—the edge of her hand against Nathan's cheek when he dozed. The street was dark. I had fallen asleep on her stoop, the pack half empty beside my hand, my bag tucked under my knees.

Hey, Olivia said.

She sat beside me, pulled two cigarettes out of the pack, and held out her hand for my lighter.

You don't smoke, I said.

Don't tell me what I do, she said, as though we were such good friends that she couldn't hurt me.

She lit both cigarettes and handed one to me.

There's something I wanted to ask you, I said.

Olivia was quiet. She took an unpracticed draw on her cigarette.

Why do you always thank Nathan? I asked. Why do you always say, *Thank you, thank you, thank you*?

What else can I say? she said. Aren't you grateful?

11

Olivia had painted me in Nathan's arms. On the canvas my hips were held up, my legs just visible on either side of his waist, arms snaked up onto the plane of his upper back, where his shoulder blades sank and protruded in the rhythm of his effort. Nathan's back: the first landscape in which his skin broke into a sweat. The scene was from the early days, I thought. Nathan's arms were not muscular but pale and undefined. Olivia had pictured us from above, our heads held close together in the forefront near the bottom of the frame, and beyond that my hands large on Nathan's back and bearing, recognizably, my rings. Nathan's face was hidden in my neck. She had concealed his face in all the paintings, which only increased their beauty and mystery. The bedding in the picture was a shadowed white, but behind us, in the top of the frame, the room swam in a deep blue. The aquatic light of Nathan's room. Olivia's brushstrokes were long and fluid, but our bodies themselves looked frozen, as though they had been suspended in stillness long enough for Olivia to represent the movement of blood and breath.

In the picture I recognized my body most acutely in its orientation toward Nathan's. My hips and calves and arms encircled him, winding their way up into the frame that had his back at its center—as though I was preparing to be lifted. The picture was painful to look at, because I could see in it that Olivia had witnessed and remembered me in total vulnerability, at a moment in which I had been undone by Nathan and unaware that she existed. Painful too because those were months, when we were first seeing one another, in which I had believed that I was separate from them. That the total surrender I saw in Olivia would not touch me.

In the gallery Olivia avoided me. I struggled to catch her eye across the room and gave it up: I knew how shy she was, how protective of her work. There was no need to embarrass her at such a victorious moment. I went outside to smoke.

It was warm on the sidewalk, and the air smelled of baked pretzels. I looked for a lighter in my bag. My body was tight with the pain of recognition, a pain that reminded me of looking at photographs of myself as an adolescent. It was tempting to forget the ugliness of transformation, bitter to remember it.

Hi, Olivia said.

She was on the sidewalk, squinting. In the sunlight her hair was almost like a creature unto itself, tentacled and thick with static. She was blushing—perhaps an inevitable state at an event designed to celebrate her.

Do you like it? she said. The picture of you?

I smiled and held my breath. I felt like a new woman who had been cut out of the aching cloth I had been before. There I was, in the paintings, being cut into shape by Nathan's attention.

It's difficult, making work about Nathan, Olivia said. She

spoke with a rush of breath, as though she were afraid of being interrupted. Because the way that I felt about it—the keenest feeling I had when we started seeing you was this kind of misery. And exhaustion. You know, it was so degrading to see how interested he was in you, how obsessed he was with fucking you. I remember one of the first nights we saw you, I was exhausted and freaked out, I went into the other room, I just left—because I needed to get back into myself, you know, it's so vulnerable in that space and I was just so tired of it—and when I came back you were fucking again! It felt awful, what Nathan wanted from me then. The way he was pushing me.

Olivia began to tie up her hair and then, almost simultaneously, to undo it again, threading her fingers through to neaten the flyaways.

But then, of course, she said, I was so grateful that he did. Grateful to be pushed like that. I feel such intense gratitude toward him—it's very profound—because he was able to bring me into all of these experiences that I'm so afraid of. But they're transformative. You, you aren't this way at all, you're so much more sexual than me, you weren't afraid of any of it, but I would never have done any of this without someone as strong as Nathan . . . with anyone except Nathan. So it's very hard to try to paint that—especially since it's sort of a secret, a secret life, and I have to respect that—to represent that process of being so afraid, of being jealous, of being neglected and hurt, even though I crave it, all that, and I want to push through.

Of course I was afraid, I said.

What were you afraid of? Olivia said. Not what you were supposed to be afraid of. Don't you think? Before the settlement, those lawyers came to me—the ones working for Leah Sabitova—and they were convinced I'd want to help put a case together. Can you imagine? Who do they think I am, who do they think Nathan is, that this is the type of fear they think I have? It's very hard, Olivia said again. Even here at the gallery there's a lot of skepticism toward Nathan—or toward the subject of the paintings, whatever they think it is. I'm sure some people suspect. They . . . you know, there are people from my childhood coming up to me, old teachers I had, friends from college, you know, asking me if I'm okay. Asking me why I'm making these kinds of paintings. I can't understand it. It seems obvious to me: I want everyone to love Nathan the way I do. Before him, when I dated other people, I was always sort of distracted. You know—I'm always in my own world, always thinking, always working. I walk around and I'm not paying attention to anything. I'm just deep in my own head, thinking about God knows what. Usually whatever I'm going to paint. And so when sex started up, a lot of the time I'd just realize I didn't have the attention for it. I was floating around, thinking about something that seemed more pressing.

But Nathan, she continued. I can't explain it—I don't even know if I've gotten at it properly. Being with him, I'm absorbed with the rhythm of it. And I don't have to worry about my body, what I'm doing, how I look or anything like that. I'm just absorbed by him, by his body. It's entirely different.

Sorry I'm telling you all of this out of the blue, Olivia said, her eyes on her shoes. She tucked her head to one side, the way she sometimes did in moments when I suspected she was humiliated. She said, I just— No one in there knows anything about any of this, about my life. Everyone's talking to me about this work as though it has something to do with them. As though they understand it.

It's scary, Liv, I said. This thing with Nathan. Because you're showing that you want something you aren't supposed to want—or that you *are* supposed to want, in this deep, mortifying way. Whether it's capitulation or rebellion, you know, you're fucked either way.

You've always known more about what we're supposed to do than I have, Olivia said. I can never keep it straight.

Olivia's eyes were darting around the sidewalk as she spoke. Then she looked at me, almost ardently. She knew. She knew, and that was why she kept secrets, why she hid her face, why she fucked in the dark. She knew the rules. Yet I could see that she was untroubled by this way in which she had learned to live in concert with desire. The gaping incongruence between her desire and her life—it was this dualism that enriched her. She accepted it. Hadn't the most important things always been private, punishable?

I thought of Nathan's apartment, the green lamps, the side table with its cavalry of glasses, and in the center of the room the bowl I imagined on Nathan's coffee table: *I need to figure it out and handle it*. Like Nathan's face in the paintings, the bowl's contents were concealed just below its edge, a visible secret that gave the image its fullness. Had I reconciled my irreconcilable lives? Or, perhaps more realistically, had I accepted their incongruence? Nathan's presence had never forced Olivia to ask this same question of herself because what I had experienced with Nathan had come from inside me. Each time I went to see him I was really going into parts of myself that I hated and craved, so that I could watch myself make the mistakes that I feared and say, *Isn't that who you really are?* But how could I even try to separate what was taught and what was instinct? It was fantasy to look for what was at my very core, for what was *me* beneath all the noise, as though there existed a sexual truth that was born in me, immune to every social lesson about what is sinister and what is sweet. At my very core were only the smallest seeds of desire, which had grown toward the directions where the light of the world guided them.

What did Nathan say? I asked Olivia. *Challenging you is not the same as violating you?* Was that it?

He does like to say that.

Are you still seeing each other?

Oh, yes.

Through the gallery window she caught the eye of a tall, clean-shaven man and nodded mildly, her cheeks that outrageous pink, before she turned on her heel and went back inside.

—

While I walked away from the gallery Nathan was at home with his wife, his hand touching her sleeve as he passed her in the kitchen, in that part of the apartment he had never shown to me. Or maybe he was beside her in bed. His watch was on his wrist, or it was on the side table where it always rested while he looked at me. He was in an elevator or a bar or a restaurant, wearing his ring, wearing his white collar, wearing his glasses. He was walking on a block the length of the block I was walking on. He was separated from me but only by a river. I felt toward him the softness you feel toward the one room in which you are allowed to be alone. How could it be that I would be happy if I never saw him again, or if I encountered him in the next minute? There was nothing rational about my feeling but I knew that when I thought I was acting rationally I was only trying to justify an inchoate desire. There was nothing rational in my feeling but it was the most generous feeling I could remember.

We love what disturbs us if it chooses us and tells us how we matter. Don't we love a cashed check, a passport, the touch of a president's hand, though each pleasure rests on a cruelty just beyond our sight? The finger points, without equivocating, at us, and we wonder at being chosen. When I thought of Nathan now I could think only of two things in tandem, never one without the other, never anything else: the richness of what he had given me and his happy, mysterious freedom, his nakedness in the bedroom uptown and right beside it the car and the open road I envisioned him driving down. His was the greatest act of service I had ever received.

ACKNOWLEDGMENTS

Thank you to my first readers: Peter Banker and Claire Schomp, for your early encouragement; David Lipsky, for your rigor and generosity, without which this book might well be moldering in a drawer; Jonathan Safran Foer, John Freeman, Zadie Smith, and Darin Strauss, for your indispensable advice; Max Addington, Corinna Anderson, Mimi Diamond, Sonia Feigelson, Hannah Kingsley-Ma, Alia Persico-Shammas, Eva Schach, and Parker Tarun, for your endurance and wisdom.

Thank you to Dan Kirschen, my champion, for your patience and lucidity; Parisa Ebrahimi, for your insight and precision; Christopher Potter and Eva Ferri, for your belief; and everyone at ICM, Curtis Brown, Hogarth, and Random House for working so hard on behalf of this book.

Thank you to my friends and co-conspirators: I love to think alongside you. Thank you to my parents, for your tremendous support and faith, which has made everything possible.

I owe the most vivid thanks of all to Phoebe Allen, for our life.

PHOTO © ANGALIS FIELD

LILLIAN FISHMAN received her MFA from NYU, where she was a Jill Davis Fellow. She lives in New York. *Acts of Service* is her first novel.